CASINO HAVANA

GRAHAM TEMPEST

BRIGHTWAY PRESS

Oliver Steele & Kon Feaver thrillers:

CASINO CARIBBEAN
CASINO DE FRANCE
CASINO HAVANA
FEAVER PITCH
JOBURG STEELE
CASINO QADDAFI

CASINO HAVANA
Brightway Press, 522 Hunt Club Blvd, Apopka, Florida 32703
ISBN (print) 978-0-9845153-9-4. bp#260513

1

I STOOD GAZING out to sea from the Malecon in Havana, the great sweeping four-mile promenade facing the ocean.

In front of me were the Florida Straits and ninety miles away, below the horizon, Key West and the United States. Behind me, the handsome but weary buildings of Havana.

Haunting my thoughts was my old friend Kon Feaver, rotting in a Cuban jail. My task: to rescue him.

The chances of success: not great.

2

———

THREE DAYS earlier I had been relaxing on the *Plage de Tahiti* at Saint-Tropez, topless capital of the world.

Kathy and I had spent the previous week in Paris. We helped prevent a terrorist from vaporising the city with a small atom bomb, so you could say we were in celebration mode.

I had taken a taxi to the Gare du Nord to return to London but then annoyed the driver by asking him to turn around and take me back to the Hotel Meurice.

Kathy and Mimi were having tea in the elegant Dali Room. Mimi is an ex-Playboy centrefold. She's also the twenty-five year old third wife of my biggest client, sixty year old Carlton Tisch.

I envy Carlton both for his millions and for his wife but my main interest is in Mimi's friend, Kathy.

Mimi smiled. "Hi, what's up?"

"Where's Carlton?" I really just wanted to see Kathy again.

"He's working."

"What are you ladies up to?"

They looked at each other. "We're going to the Riviera for a few days," said Mimi.

"Saint-Tropez," said Kathy. "We're in France, after all."

Mimi and Kathy are the same age and the same height and build. Both are knockouts by any standard. Mimi is dark haired and Kathy blonde but they could be sisters.

They share a waspish sense of humour, meaning they discuss people behind their backs with relish. 'People' includes me. Their closeness has led some to suggest there's something physical going on and I wonder about that, but if so they are discreet about it. Both have relationships with men – Mimi with her husband and Kathy with me.

"Come too," said Mimi. "Carlton has to fly home but Mike Kalestian is in town. He may join us."

Kalestian is a friend of Carlton's but younger, about thirty-five. He owns casinos in Las Vegas and Macau. He's a brash bounder with flashing eyes and a big moustache who works out and wears Speedos. I don't like him.

I rubbed my chin. "Not sure I can spare the time."

"Go on," said Mimi. "It'll be fun."

So after much deliberation I found room in my busy schedule.

"I'M NOT LOOKING FORWARD to being ogled by Kalestian the Speedo king," said Kathy.

We were in a small hotel down by Saint-Tropez Harbour, in a room overlooking the fishing boats.

Besides being cute Kathy is sharp witted, more so than me, which is a turn-on. She also speaks her mind. I've been told I'm prejudiced in favour of strong women. Guilty as charged. She's five foot seven and nicely rounded, with gleaming fair hair, a tee shirt and jeans person, not *haute couture*.

"You don't like him, do you?" she said.

"No."

She sat at the dressing table combing her blonde hair, wet from the shower. She had teamed up tee shirt-wise with Superbowl winner Tom Brady. Tom's handsome mug beamed from a 100% pre-shrunk cotton number that did nothing to cover her legs.

"You have great legs," I said.

"I do, don't I," she said.

4

AT THE BEACH we undressed down to our swimsuits. Kathy's white bikini offset her golden tan.

"Keep going," I said.

She gave me a look between amused and annoyed and peeled off her bra.

Mimi hesitated which was interesting because before she married Carlton she had posed for a Playboy spread that went well beyond topless, but she followed suit.

Once we were oiled and sipping our drinks, Kalestian asked me, "Where's your friend Kon?"

"Florida. He had a run to make."

"A run?"

"To Cuba."

Kon is a free spirit who runs a boat service from Cuba to Florida for refugees who want to make a new life in the United States. He keeps a sturdy forty foot cruiser at his home on Coquina Key. His knowledge of the lonely stretch of islands and causeways running from Key Largo to Key West makes him a formidable guide.

"So he's a coyote?" asked Kalestian. He used the derogatory term for a people smuggler.

"Absolutely not," said Kathy. "Coyotes take huge fees. Kon just charges for gas plus something to live on."

Mimi's mobile phone rang.

"Hi Carlton," she said.

"Hold on."

She handed me the phone. "Speak of the devil. It's about Kon."

"Hi, Carlton."

"Kon's been arrested."

I was shocked and also surprised. It was true that smuggling people was illegal in both Cuba and the United States but Cuba was not as concerned as it once was about refugees. And at the U.S. end, Kon was adept at finding remote spots in the Keys to unload his passengers, so his risk of being caught there was minimal.

"How serious is it?"

"He's in a Cuban jail."

"How come?"

"We're trying to find out. I guess there was a

tipoff because when Kon got to the pickup point the Cuban police were there in force."

"Is he okay?"

A pause. "Bruno thinks he was badly beaten up." Bruno was Kon's contact in Havana.

That was the end of my Riviera vacation. The accountant in me said I should finish my spell at the beach and then return to my home in Coconut Grove to await news. But I just couldn't.

Kon is a good friend, although he's about as different from me as a person can be. He's a genial ex-Israeli fighter pilot and recovering alcoholic who played soccer for Tel Aviv, was tossed out of the Israeli Air Force for excessive drinking and then roamed the world as a mercenary before getting into people-smuggling.

I by contrast am an accountant, the product of a pricy British education, not noted for my wide emotional range. I'm not ashamed of that, in fact I'm proud of it.

So Kon and I are polar opposites.

But I had to help him.

5

"Why were you carrying Sanchez Madera?"

In Cienfuegos, Cuba, sometimes known as the Pearl of the South, an individual with a scarred face and a personality to match stood in front of Kon Feaver, who was tied to a chair.

Kon spat out a tooth. "Who's Sanchez Madera?"

"He was waiting to board your boat."

"I don't know anything about that."

The man punched him savagely in the stomach.

6

In his office in Cienfuegos, Police Commander Hector Cruz was reading the Miami Herald on his laptop.

The 'phone rang.

"Yes?"

"This is Marco. We're getting nowhere with the American."

"I told you not to use that term."

"The prisoner then."

"What's the problem?"

"He's very stubborn."

"You may have to put him in *la caja*."

There was a pause. "I don't know if that'll work. It's a slow process and you said you wanted quick results."

Cruz's black hair shone with gel. He was pale

skinned and his short black beard was trimmed to a point. His otherwise handsome face was marred by a permanent frown.

He wore the blue and grey uniform of an officer in the PNR, the Policía Nacional Revolucionaria. The uniform looked drab on most people but on his muscular frame the neatly pressed grey shirt with epaulettes and badges of rank on the shoulders was quite flattering.

The senior officer in a police territory covering two provinces, at the age of forty his clean-cut looks and humourless manner had served him well as a fast-rising star – he came across as a dedicated agent of the state who would enforce the law without pity.

La caja – the box – was a tiny cell four feet square and three feet high in which it was impossible to stand or sit in comfort. After a few hours the pain in the subject's limbs and joints became intense. He would twist and turn in a futile attempt at relief. Prisoners were often left there for weeks in extreme heat with minimal slops for food and no toilet. Occasionally the door would be opened briefly to sluice the subject down and remove the dirt and excrement.

"Put him there anyway. It'll soften him up." He went back to reading about Cuba's First Vice President, Miguel Díaz-Canel.

The uncensored availability of the Herald, no

supporter of the Castros, reflected the changing times. Since Fidel turned the presidency over to his brother Raul, things had relaxed slightly. Raul, eighty-five himself, had indicated he would not run for office in 2018, so this was a sort of interim period, post-Fidel and pre . . . pre what, exactly?

That was the question. What did the next few years hold? And among the ambitious, who would advance?

Raul's pending retirement had turned the spotlight on Díaz-Canel, an engineer by training and supposedly progressive. The man had played his cards well, thought Cruz cynically. He had managed not to be perceived as a rival to the Castros, unlike other contenders now in prison or dead, so he seemed well placed to succeed to the presidency.

But not if Cruz had anything to do with it. He was thirteen years younger than the vice president. That meant that, unless he could jump ahead, he was in for a long wait. Some would have been content to wait their turn but not Cruz.

He finished reading and switched off the computer.

He had been successful so far, which was reflected in his surroundings. The house was built in the 1920's as the beach home of a wealthy sugar growing family but was confiscated when Castro took power. The second floor room was spacious, its wood floor waxed until it gleamed, paintings by modern Cuban artists Rafael Martinez and Wilfredo Lam lining the walls.

But past success was not enough. The rest of his plan must be executed rigorously. And one of Kon Feaver's passengers was a major threat to that plan.

AFTER SPEAKING TO CRUZ, the jailer Marco beckoned to an associate and together they left the small concrete block cabin that served as an office and strolled across the sand to the prison yard.

Cayo Piedra was a prison island. Few Cubans even knew of its existence.

The island was barely a mile long. The prison consisted of two single storey buildings, each with a dozen cells, standing on opposite sides of a square. The yard was bordered by a twenty foot high chain link fence topped with razor wire. In the centre was a watchtower tall enough for the guards to overlook both cell blocks.

A couple of guards lounged in the tower, rifles slung from their shoulders. When they saw Marco emerge from the office outside the fence they straightened up and one of them came down to let him and his companion into the compound.

Marco did not show much sense of caution. He was unarmed. Only a few cells were occupied. In the entire life of the prison there had never been a successful escape, such was the remoteness of the island and the brutality with which occasional attempts were punished.

One such punishment was about to be applied. They approached a cell, unlocked it and went inside.

"GET HIM UP," said Marco.

Kon was sitting on the earth floor with his back propped against the wall. He was hungry and thirsty and his face was a mess of cuts and bruises. The midday heat was overpowering with no breeze to cool the cells. He had little reason for hope of rescue or even easy treatment so his spirits were low but when he heard the key turn and saw the door open, he determined not to show it and straightened up slightly.

The guard pulled Kon upright.

The Israeli could barely stand unaided. He wiped blood and sweat from his face.

"I'll ask again," said Marco. "Why were you carrying Sanchez Madera?" His English was crude and accented but his voice was calm, almost sympathetic.

"I told you, I have no idea. He was someone who paid for a place on my boat, nothing more. I don't ask about the personal lives of my passengers."

Marco shook his head sadly. He motioned to the guard.

"Take him."

He returned to his office, and telephoned Cruz.

"He's in *la caja*. But his attitude is poor. Don't expect quick results."

At the other end of the line, Cruz grunted and hung up. He stared out of the window, thought for a moment and then telephoned a number in the United States.

THE MOBILE PHONE rang in the pocket of Stanley Rothman, in a top floor conference room at the massive Portofino Resort in Las Vegas.

"It's Cruz, Mr. Rothman."

"What d'you want?" Rothman's voice was gruff. He excused himself and walked out onto the balcony for privacy. It was quiet there apart from the low hum of traffic on Las Vegas Boulevard far below.

"We're sweating the prisoner to learn more about Sanchez Madera."

"Will that work?"

"It always does eventually."

"Keep me posted."

"Yes, sir."

Cruz's tone was respectful, reflecting the unequal relationship. He was a supplicant deferring to his backer. Rothman owned the Portofino, along with its clone in Macau and several other casinos.

He was in the middle of a meeting with Diana Jacobs, a partner in the accounting firm that audited his business. They were discussing the company's financial statements.

He was a short man in his early eighties. There was a carefully cultivated spring in his step but telltale signs – the red in his thin hair fighting a losing battle with the grey, and large liver spots on his pale forehead – gave the game away. Even in the sunshine he wore a suit with the jacket buttoned against chills. He went back inside.

"Well, Madam Auditor, what's your bottom line?"

She smiled. She was well aware that Rothman, who she found repulsive, still fancied himself a ladies man. Her youth and good looks had been factors in her company assigning her this account and she felt she should be liberal with her flattery. "You made a lot of money last year."

He frowned. "Save the compliments my dear, what I pay you for is frank advice."

"Fair enough. Then let me point out some areas of concern."

"Go ahead."

"Your Macau casino is profitable but this handsome resort here in Las Vegas barely breaks even."

Rothman nodded. "Go on."

"It's not alone, of course. Half the resorts on the Strip are in the same boat."

"How do I fix that?"

"I'm not sure you can."

"Raise prices?"

She shook her head. "Too much competition. Casinos on Indian land. Internet gambling. And prices here already reflect that today's Las Vegas is a luxury destination."

Rothman nodded. "That's why I invested in Macau."

"Which has bailed you out handsomely."

"Yes, it's been a cash cow."

"Long may that last," said Jacobs.

But there was a fly in the ointment and they both knew it. Much of Macau's early profits had come from criminals laundering their illegal income. Then China's anticorruption President Xi Jinping cracked down and cash flow fell off dramatically.

"You're going to need another trick soon," said Jacobs.

"I may have one."

"Really?"

Rothman nodded. "That call I just took was from Cuba. What if I told you that one day soon there will be casinos in Havana again and I shall be the biggest investor there?"

Jacobs looked doubtful. She recognised the

exotic appeal of the island nation and Havana's gaudy history as a gaming mecca pre-Castro, with tales of the Mafia, prostitution and high life. But those days were long gone. True, relations with the United States had eased recently but the boycott was still in place. The prospect of U.S. investment in casinos, an industry forbidden fifty years ago under Castro was, in her private opinion, a pipe dream.

"Do you see things changing?" she asked.

"Yes. And when they do I shall have an inside track."

"How so?"

"I'm financing the next President of Cuba."

I CALLED my boss Carlton Tisch in New York.

"What's happening?" he asked.

"I don't really know where to start," I said.

He was in his so-called office – an elegant town-house on East 62nd Street – having breakfast at the mahogany dining table, the one that magically turned into a conference table if the IRS threatened to visit.

A word about Carlton. He's a grumpy piece of work who doesn't suffer fools gladly. He started with nothing and is now worth north of a billion dollars. His parents ran a small deli on the Lower East Side and there was no college money for young Carl, but he got a job in the mail room at Goldman Sachs. Within a year he persuaded Goldman to back the takeover of an ailing debt finance company with himself as president. Talk about hustle. He now owns Eastern Debt Factors, the largest firm of its kind in the eastern states.

He's slow to put his hand in his pocket when it comes time to pay for a round but he's not as mean as he likes to pretend. I've seen his tax returns and the amount he gives to charity every year is more than I earn in a decade.

Carlton and Kon Feaver go back a long way. He trusts Kon. When he doesn't want to admit owner-ship of some fishy venture he puts it in Kon's name. There's no formal contract, just trust. Divorce lawyers for both his ex-wives attest to the power of the arrangement.

"Call Kon's contact in Havana, this guy Bruno," he snapped. "That's who I spoke to."

Bruno is a fixer. He's useful to Kon at the Cuban end, lining up passengers. Kon likes him but doesn't trust him.

I phoned Bruno. The line from Saint-Tropez was surprisingly clear.

"Bruno, this is Oliver Steele, a friend of Kon."

"Hi, Mr. Oliver."

"Just Oliver. What happened that night? Were you there?"

"Yes, but truly Mr. Oliver, I could not prevent it."

"Just Oliver, Bruno. It's okay, we're not blaming you. Tell me what happened."

"We were at a beach in Matanzas, twenty kilometres east of Havana."

I had the map of Cuba open on my laptop. Matanzas was shown in black capitals, a province somewhat east of Havana. I switched to Wikipedia.

"I see Matanzas. Apparently it has excellent beaches."

"That's why we use it. There's a place where Kon can bring his boat close to the shore. He uses a rubber dinghy to transfer the passengers."

"What's your part in the process?"

"I monitor the weather – the operation needs a calm night and no moon. I also assemble the passengers, usually between six and twenty people, and bring them from Havana in my van."

"You have a place in Havana?"

"Yes. It's a house I use for . . ." He paused.

"For what?"

"Another business."

Bruno ran a black market warehouse. If you needed a toaster that cost thirty dollars in the States, Bruno would sell it to you for fifty, but you would be lucky to find one at all in a government store. People like Bruno were a significant part of the Cuban economy, acting as a bridge between the needs of the individual and a state system that fell way short of meeting them. But if he wanted to be coy about how he made a living, okay.

"Go on," I said.

"That evening, the passengers found their way to my office in Havana as usual. I put them in the van and drove to Matanzas."

"How much did you know about them?"

"I knew their money was good."

"I thought nobody had money in Cuba. How did they pay?"

"Some had CUPs, some had CUCs. Others paid in dollars."

CUPs and CUCs were the two parallel currencies used in Cuba. CUP meant the Cuban peso and CUC the convertible peso, tied to the dollar. It's an awkward system that Fidel introduced in the nineties to preserve precious hard currency.

"Dollars? You have a dollar account?"

He hesitated. "Not in Cuba. I have an arrangement in . . . another place."

I guessed he meant a Caribbean tax haven – possibly Tortola where Carlton lived, or the Caymans. Grand Cayman, about two hundred miles south of Cuba would be a convenient choice for someone with a boat. My understanding of Bruno's grey netherworld was broadening.

"What happened then?"

"Once in Matanzas I drove out along the coast road to our beach. It was a calm evening as I said, no moon. Kon was coming from Florida, we had arranged to meet at nine. He's a good seaman and usually punctual.

"Things seemed fine at first. The passengers were waiting, each with one bag like on the airlines. Kon's boat arrived, without lights and moving as quietly as possible. It dropped anchor – he uses a light anchor but it bites into the sand pretty well – and he pushed the inflatable raft over the side.

"He was loading the first passengers when things went crazy. A large launch roared in, its searchlight sweeping around. It blocked Kon's boat from getting away. A bunch of uniformed men emerged from the bushes."

"Armed?"

"Of course."

"What were they – police, coastguard?"

"They were PNR."

"PNR?"

"Policia Nacional Revolucionaria. The regular police. You could see their uniforms in the glare – grey shirts and blue trousers, standard police kit."

"Whereabouts were you?"

"I was in my van."

"What did you do?"

"I slid down in the seat, hoping not to be seen. But a sergeant came and hauled me out of there."

"How come you are here to tell the tale?"

He shrugged. "They let me go. It sounds odd, I

know. But smuggling people out of Cuba is not a huge deal nowadays. They book you, of course, and you have to go to court. For a first offence you probably get a warning and pay a fine."

"Is that all?"

"Sure. I don't think they care. If a few people make it across the Straits and reach dry land, so what? Once they get settled, they will send dollars back to their families in Cuba. Everybody wins."

"That's why this raid is surprising. Why all the drama?" I asked.

"Beats me." He didn't sound too interested.

"Doesn't it suggest they were looking for somebody? Not Kon, someone else?"

"Maybe."

"It also sounds as if they expected you guys would be there."

"I guess."

"How could they have known that?" I asked.

"Maybe somebody tipped them off."

"How could that happen?"

"I don't know. It wasn't me."

"What happened then?"

"The passengers scattered. They were trying to get away. They ran in all directions. The police chased them and here's the thing: they caught all but one of them. Out of six passengers they caught five and brought them back. One guy got away."

"Smart of him."

"Yeah, but there were a lot of sand dunes and a lot of bushes. And the ocean itself, perhaps he just swam out to sea. Maybe he drowned. Whatever, they didn't catch him. And they were pretty mad when they came back, so he could be the one you're talking about, the one they really wanted."

"What was his name?"

"Martin. A college professor, I think. Like I say, they didn't get him."

I tried to discern a trail I could follow. "This Martin. How did he pay?"

"In dollars."

"From where?"

Bruno hesitated as if not understanding. "I forget."

"You must have records."

"Just a minute." Sounding cross he left the phone and came back a minute later. "I received wired funds from the Bank of A. Spiro on Tortola."

The name rang a bell. Spiro was a small bank but I knew of it and had used it occasionally. It was known for flexibility. Carlton Tisch had done business with them too and he handled much bigger bucks than I, so we might have an introduction there.

"Does it mention the sender's name?"

"No. Just the amount, five thousand dollars."

"Five thousand? Kon charges much less."

I knew Kon only charged his passengers three thousand, far below the market rate for people-smuggling, a business which traditionally gouged passengers for every last penny. The going rate was twelve grand. I could have dropped the matter, but annoyance got the better of me.

He sounded whiny. "I have expenses. And the risk is great."

I didn't want to start a fight. It was more important to find Kon. "Go on."

"It was odd. Why the police? The Coastguard I could understand, but the police?"

"Here's a theory," I said. "Someone had it in for this guy Martin but didn't want folk to see what they were up to, so they planned this raid on their own. They set you free because they didn't want it becoming a news item. They wanted things kept quiet."

"So it wasn't a real government operation? But the police were there!"

"It could have been planned by someone in the police who had a private agenda."

"What sort of agenda?"

"Who knows? Financial, political, a mixture?"

"Beats me, buddy," he said.

I nodded although he couldn't see me. "Damn right, buddy."

I CALLED TISCH AGAIN.

"Bruno doesn't know where Kon is but he gave me a lead to a guy who was involved in the raid and got away. He paid his passage with a draft from the Bank of A. Spiro."

Tisch laughed. "Honest Abe!"

"You use him, don't you?"

"Not lately. Abe Spiro will do anything if the price is right."

"Oh dear me."

"Don't be cute," said Tisch. "I prefer to do business with people with impeccable ethics."

"Nowadays," I said.

"What's that supposed to mean?"

"Sounds like the old businessman's motto: Get on, get honour, get honest."

Tisch has a sense of humour, he's too smart not to, but I wouldn't call it elastic. "What do you need from me?" he snapped.

"An introduction to Spiro. I want to know who paid for the mystery man's passage to Florida. You have leverage so please call him. You can let him think there's some business coming his way."

"What sort of business?"

"I don't know. How about a fat foreign exchange transaction at his standard commission?"

"Forget it. He would want one percent and I never pay above a quarter."

"You needn't do it, just say you're thinking about it."

"I'll think about it."

APPARENTLY CARLTON WAS able to bend his moral code because Abe Spiro greeted me like a long lost friend.

Which was just as well because when I walked into his comfortable office in Road Town I was pretty groggy. I had flown from Paris via London to Antigua which alone took sixteen hours. The plane was late reaching Antigua, so I missed the connecting flight to Tortola. I caught the ferry to Soper's Hole instead, rented a Jeep and, half awake, negotiated Tortola's corkscrew goat paths across the island trying hard not to drive off the road.

Spiro was tanned and grey haired, pushing seventy, and wore a crisp white shirt and a Haileybury tie. He shook my hand vigorously and poured us each a gin and tonic.

He spoke perfect BBC English.

"For some reason I thought you were American," I said.

He laughed and shook his head. "English and Greek. Born and raised in Hampstead. My wife's American, maybe that's what you had in mind. My father-in-law set me up in the banking business. I still do the odd deal but I'm semi-retired. I sail, play a bit of squash and generally enjoy island life."

I explained about Kon. "I'm short of leads. I want to learn more about this character Martin who is on the run from the Cuban police."

Spiro blinked but he made no bones about it. He pulled out the records and studied them.

"His name is Martin Sanchez Madera. He's actually rather a fine person. He's an academic but also a frustrated journalist and politician. Neither of which are good things to be in Cuba unless you admire the Castros, which he does not. I don't know why he was on your friend's boat but it probably had something to do with his commitment to restoring democracy in Cuba."

"How are you involved?"

"When I'm in Miami I play golf with Pedro Macias, the son of Hugo."

I recognised the names. The older Macias was a freedom fighter with Fidel Castro but disapproved of Castro's turn to communism. Fidel arrested him and threw him in prison for twenty years for betraying the revolution – the usual excuse. After years of torture and privation Macias sought exile in Florida and was now prominent in the émigré community.

"Do you do business with Pedro?"

"We do a few deals, mostly real estate. Two years ago he asked me to open an account for Sanchez Madera. The funds came from the Macias family so presumably Hugo and Pedro Macias support Martin's political activity."

"I would think so."

"Pedro, particularly, is active in Cuban affairs."

"What does that mean?"

"Fund raising, public speaking. There are also rumours . . . " He hesitated.

"Rumours?"

"That he is training commandos in the Everglades."

"With a view to what? Not another invasion, surely? The Bay of Pigs was a fiasco, both military and political."

"Who knows?"

I filed that away for future reference.

"By the way," he said, "Carlton knows the Macias family. You should get him to arrange a meeting."

I got up to leave. "Thanks, you've been really helpful."

He shrugged. "I know I broke a confidence but, if

Martin is in trouble, what you're doing may help him."

"You will be rewarded," I said. "Carlton talked about sending some business your way."

He smiled. "I won't hold my breath. Carlton's a great guy but I know a come-on when I hear one. You can't kid a kidder. "

I called Tisch in Miami. "You never said you knew Pedro Macias."

"I know a lot of people."

"I want to meet him."

He thought briefly. "Lunch tomorrow. The Forge on Miami Beach."

Carlton can move fast when he wants to, which is fine but it meant more travelling for me.

13

"JUST HOLD ON," Kon told himself in *la caja*.

He had been unconscious. He had no idea how many hours he had been in the box but it was growing dark now and it had been the middle of the day when they shut him in. His eyes had grown accustomed to the gloom – a few cracks admitted faint light. The heat, overpowering at first, was still intense.

His head ached and his face felt flushed. He wondered if his body temperature was climbing. He had read somewhere that heat stroke occurred when your temperature rose to a certain level and went on rising at an accelerating rate; it was fatal if not addressed in time. The treatment was to wrap you in ice and spray you with freezing water. Fat chance of that happening here.

He grunted in pain as his legs spasmed with piercing cramps. The muscles in his knotted calves felt as if they were being stretched to snapping point and it was all he could do not to scream. Lying on his side in a semi-foetal position, he tried to stretch but banged his feet on the wooden sides of the box. It was like being in a coffin, a comparison he tried to dismiss – there was an ominous finality to the thought.

The cramps passed after what felt like minutes but was probably just a few seconds. He knew they would come back, and worse because of the dehydration.

His spine ached, something separate. It felt like hot irons clamped to the small of his back. Nothing 600 milligrams of Ibuprofen wouldn't fix, he thought drily.

At some point he lost consciousness again.

AT THE FORGE RESTAURANT, I shook hands with Hugo Macias, father of Pedro.

"It's an honour," I said. "I didn't know you would be here."

By sprinting through various airports – Tortola, San Juan, and Miami – I had reached the restaurant, breathless but in time for lunch.

Our meeting at the Forge was an example of Carlton's dry humour. The elegant restaurant on Arthur Godfrey Road used to be a favourite of Meyer Lansky, accountant to the Mob and a major investor in Cuban casinos before the fall of Batista.

It has changed owners since then. What hasn't changed is that it's still very expensive. You feel it as soon as you approach the grey stone facade with its glass canopy and gleaming brass lanterns. A magnum of Cristal will set you back $1,500. Still, Carlton was paying.

He was already there with Pedro and Hugo. Hugo was bald and shrunken – his shirt seemed too large round the neck – but he had a sweet smile that lit up his face.

"My dad will go a long way for a free meal," joked Pedro. He jumped up and shook my hand. He had a grin that radiated good nature and optimism. Although only medium height, he had broad muscular shoulders under a pink polo shirt. Abe Spiro had mentioned that he was a college football star and could also drive a golf ball 300 yards on the fly and from the strength of his grip I could believe it. I think he relaxed his grasp halfway through our handshake.

"Let's eat," growled Carlton, who likes his food.

The conversation soon turned serious.

"I know your first question," said Pedro. "What was Martin Sanchez Madera doing on your friend's boat? Well, he was coming to see my dad and me."

"Why?"

"He is committed to instituting democracy in Cuba, which is our goal also. He was making the dangerous trip to meet us and plan opposition to the regime."

"Tell me about him," I said.

"He teaches economics at Havana University. He

is smart, fluent in English, part-academic, part-politician and part-frustrated journalist. "

"He sounds impressive."

Pedro nodded. "In the States he might have become a Congressman or in your country a Member of Parliament. But in Cuba such people have problems."

"How old is he?"

"He's only thirty. He has made rapid progress as a professor but the more he teaches, the more he realises it's impossible to avoid speaking the truth about his own country."

"Meaning?"

"They say the truth will set you free but in Cuba it's the opposite. The truth can get you locked up – and that's if you're lucky. It may get you shot."

"What exactly does he do?"

"He's making plans for life after Castro, quietly building relationships outside Cuba with people like us. He has written papers outlining ways to transition to democracy and identifying people who could be part of the new order."

"A shadow government for when the time comes?"

"Exactly."

"Let me guess," I said. "In the course of doing all this he has knocked heads with a few bad guys."

Pedro nodded grimly. "And how! He was coming here to discuss certain difficulties."

"Do you think one of those difficulties – or people – tripped him up?" asked Carlton. He seemed to like Pedro. Perhaps he appreciated the younger man's practical approach. Pedro had mentioned that he did not finish university, dropping out to work on a real estate deal that made him a lot of money. Carlton never went to university either, and could be hard on people who had.

"It's possible."

"I understand why you want to overthrow the Castros," I said. "They stole so much from you. Do you plan to seek compensation?"

Macias Senior had been listening. He shook his head quietly.

There was an embarrassed silence, broken by Pedro.

"That is not my father's case. He was a farmer, comfortably off but not rich."

Hugo smiled. "Do you know the computer programme called Google Maps?"

"Of course."

"Sometimes I look on Google Maps and I can see my old house and our farm in Oriente. It makes me homesick, but I shall never go back, it's too late now. However, after sixty years of dictatorship and repression I'd like to see something at least resembling democracy."

"And you think Sanchez Madera offers that?"

"He's Cuba's best hope."

After the meal we all shook hands. As we were leaving I had a chance to buttonhole Pedro. "I've heard some interesting rumours about you."

"Really?"

"Something about training commandos in the Everglades."

The grin broadened. "The things people say."

"Is it true?"

"What do you think?"

We reached the parking lot and he stopped by a big black Cadillac. "This is my dad's car."

He wished us luck and helped his father into the gleaming vehicle that would take him back to his home in Hialeah.

So he didn't confirm the rumour, but he didn't deny it either.

15

"WHAT ARE YOUR PLANS?" Tisch asked.

He was heading home to Tortola to join Mimi and Kathy, which meant a flight via San Juan, Puerto Rico. We were sharing a taxi to the airport.

We cruised west on Arthur Godfrey, then north on Le Jeune.

"You know me. When in doubt, march towards the sound of the guns."

"That's what I was afraid of. With so little information to work with, isn't that foolhardy?"

"A little."

"You don't speak Spanish."

"I do, a few words. The British have been vacationing in Spain for decades and I spent time there in my student days."

"What about a visa? They're hard to get."

"For Americans, sure. But I have dual nationality and a British passport. I'll fly via Canada. When I buy my ticket at Toronto Airport the airline will give me a Cuban Travel Card. It's actually a visa good for thirty days. That should be enough."

"What about money? You can't use credit cards."

"Sure you can. Just not American ones."

Tisch was not a man to be put off. "Who will help you there?"

"Bruno."

"That flake?"

"He's all we've got."

"You will be in a dangerous environment, with only a black market fixer to help you."

"Good point. I'll have to watch him."

"You'll also be fighting the authorities."

"True."

"You won't be able to call on the good guys for help because you don't know who they are."

"Pretty dire," I agreed.

"So?"

"But," I said.

"But what?"

"Do you have a better idea?"

16

"ENCANTADO," I said.

I held out my hand.

Bruno shook it firmly. "Encantado. Welcome to Havana, Mr. Oliver."

I've found over the years that a firm handshake isn't always good. Sometimes the shaker is a four-square guy, but other times he's thinking something really devious and doesn't want you to know it.

He looked me straight in the eye – also not a good sign – and smiled. The smile was warm and humorous but did not quite reach his eyes which stayed fixed on mine. A salesman's smile. He ran a black market consumer goods store, after all.

I saw a clean-shaven young man, medium height, in khakis and a navy Ralph Lauren polo shirt. He was suntanned, his glossy black hair in a modified mohawk shaved close to the scalp on both sides but standing up proudly in the middle.

I always wonder, when I see that kind of hairdo, how long does it take to trim? It must need pruning daily or the sides would get shaggy. A guy who spends that much time on his appearance must be a bit vain. Just my opinion.

Fresh-faced, open, uncomplicated, easy to like, Kon had said, picking his words with care. Easy to like but not to trust? I'd have to figure that out for myself.

"And you speak Spanish. That is excellent. I speak the good English so we're AOK, no?"

I was relieved. I can say hello in a dozen languages but after that my vocabulary runs out fast. Bruno might mangle his syntax a bit but even so, communicating in English would make life a whole lot easier.

"And you have excellent taste, to stay in this historic place."

We were in the lobby of the Ambos Mundos Hotel. The Ambos Mundos, although famous, had been a borderline choice. The reviews were luke-warm like the so-called hot water in my bedroom but it was good enough for Ernest Hemingway so staying there checked a box for me. Ernest had lived there in 1939 when he moved to Cuba with Martha Gelhorn. Later he bought Finca Vigia, a comfortable estate a little way out of town where he married Martha, drank, divorced, got married again, wrote 'For Whom the Bell Tolls,' supported Castro's overthrow of Batista and suffered severe depression before returning to the States and shooting himself at sixty-one.

This morning the Ambos Mundos seemed to be living off its association with the Old Man because the service was slow and the staff indifferent.

"Can we go somewhere else?" I asked.

He took me to a bar down the road and offered me a *Mojito* but it was a bit early in the day and I wanted to keep a clear head. He ordered one himself and I sipped a cola of unknown origin.

"Where do we start?" I asked. "Do you have any idea where Kon might be?"

He shook his head. "I last saw him being bundled into a police van along with five others and driven off into the night."

"But you yourself were spared?"

He gave me a strange look. "I was just the driver. I was of no interest to them."

His English had gone from stilted to faultless. As if he had rehearsed his reply.

"Five passengers, not six? You say the sixth man got away?"

"That's right."

"What about the other five, are they still missing?"

"Actually, no. They were released the next day."

"And you know that how?"

He laughed. "They all called me, very upset, demanding passage on another boat."

Or wanting their money back, I thought. "And is that something you can arrange?"

"Probably. I'll use Sinbad."

"Sinbad?"

"My backup to Kon." He sounded defensive.

I said, "I'm interested in the sixth man. What do you know about him?"

"As I told you, I knew only his name, or at least the name he gave me. And that his money was good."

"What name did he give you?"

"Martin."

"Martin who?"

"Just Martin."

He saw my expression. "You think I'm inefficient? That my record keeping is too casual?"

"Well . . ."

"If you lived here you would understand. What if I kept perfect records? Suppose I am raided and my papers are taken?" He shook his head. "It's not a game, all this."

"I know his full name," I said.

"Tell me."

"He is Martin Sanchez Madera. He's a professor at the university. I want you to help me find him."

"You think he can help?"

"It's the only lead we have."

"We can go back to my place and look him up."

"Where's your house?"

"Just west of the Old City. A short walk."

We strolled down Calle Obispo to Paseo de Marti, the Prado. Gazing round, I was struck by the handsome lines of the grey stone buildings, weathered but elegant. Bruno pointed out a building that looked to me like the Capitol in Washington D.C. and I remarked on the resemblance.

"This one is taller actually," said Bruno. "It's the Capitolio, formerly Cuba's seat of government. It houses the Ministry of Science and Technology now."

Then came the Gran Teatro de la Habana. "One of the world's largest opera houses," he said proudly. In a parking lot opposite the Teatro stood a flock of wonderful, dignified old Detroit cars from the 1950's with wavy fins and breast-like bumpers, aristocrats of their class. Polished till they caught the sun like mirrors, their owners leaned against their lacquered flanks, chatting and waiting patiently for tourists.

Finally we passed the Hotel Inglaterra, another Spanish-inspired grey stone pile. "That's where

José Marti used to hang out and preach separation from Spain, prior to the War of Independence of 1895."

We turned onto Calle Trocadero.

"How did you find his name?" Bruno asked.

"From the financial information you gave me." I didn't elaborate. The fewer people who knew about Sanchez Madera and his activities the better and I still wasn't sure about Bruno.

The streets of the old city were narrow and winding. Decades of salt air and burning sun had worn away curlicues and flourishes once sharply pointed, lending a weathered patina that was agreeably mellow, but crumbling, and it was apparently years since they had seen a coat of paint.

We came to a drab two storey house in a quiet street. An old but clean van stood in the yard – the van that had taken the passengers to Matanzas? Bruno let us into the house through the back door.

The downstairs rooms were jam packed with glossy cartons containing the sort of consumer goods – television sets, kitchen appliances and the like – deemed essential by middle class Western society. A table in one corner was piled high with wooden cigar boxes bearing famous labels – Partagas, Romeo y Julieta and Montecristo. Another room contained nothing but ceramic bathroom tiles in a range of colours.

"Where does all this stuff come from?" I indicated the tiles.

"Mexico."

"How did you get them?"

He just shrugged.

"I've heard that state employees earn as little as $25 a month," I said. "Is that true?

"Yes."

"So how can they afford Mexican tiles?"

"They can't. But there are two separate economies in Cuba."

"You mean CUCs and CUPs?"

"That's part of it. But it's really about two different sets of consumers. There are the state employees you mentioned, who earn next to nothing. And then there are the private sector people. Those are my customers."

"And their money comes from abroad?"

He nodded. "Tourism. Most tourists have no idea of the value of their money. They don't understand that when they tip a dollar here, it's like giving ten. In rural areas and poor parts of town, food costs a fraction of what you pay in bars and hotels."

"With all the money you are making, you could afford to paint the outside of this house," I said. I was joking but he took me seriously.

"That would not be wise. It would attract attention – from burglars, jealous rivals, officials looking for a bribe. I keep a low profile."

"Oh, okay."

"Anyway, come up to the office."

The upstairs rooms were just as crowded, but the contents were different. There were rolled-up carpets and many bolts of cloth for curtains or suiting. A tiny office in one bedroom had room for a table and chair and a metal filing cabinet, padlocked.

Bruno consulted a dog-eared phone book and dialled a number. He unleashed a stream of rapid Spanish then turned to me. "You're in luck. He's lecturing right now at the main University campus. He should be finished in half an hour. It's across town, not far. Let's go there and talk to the guy."

"Just like that?"

"Sure, why not? I know what he looks like. We'll bump into him by accident, it's the best way."

17

"SEÑOR MARTIN," I shouted as politely as I could.

We were standing outside a lecture hall on the spacious university campus, watching a line of young people straggle out of the auditorium. We had taken a taxi and I noticed that the money handed over by Bruno and accepted without comment by the driver was way less than what I would have expected from my guide book.

A tall young man turned towards us with a half-smile of enquiry. Broad brow and unruly shock of hair gave him a passing resemblance to the young President Kennedy.

"Questions?"

"We aren't in the class," said Bruno. "We just want to chat."

Sanchez Madera recognised Bruno and his expression changed from humour to wariness.

I stepped forward. "Pedro and Hugo Macias say hi."

His face froze. "Who are you?"

"My name is Steele. I've just come from Miami where I met Pedro Macias and his father. They said I should look you up."

He stared at me with an intensity that was startling because it was so unexpected and I sensed the calculating brain behind his mild appearance. Finally he jerked his head. "Over there."

Across the way was a large space of green lawn with some benches, mostly empty. The crowd of students leaving the lecture hall was thinning out, but he waited until there was nobody remotely within hearing.

"Now, please explain yourself."

"The skipper of your boat was arrested by the police, and hasn't been seen since. Happens he's a friend of mine. I was hoping you could help me find him."

Sanchez Madera seemed to reach a conclusion about me because his frown softened and was replaced by an easy charm. I recalled that Pedro Macias had described him as part politician.

"I guess I'll accept your bona fides, since you know about that crazy evening. But how did you trace me? I try to leave a light footprint. Even Bruno here didn't know my full name."

Bruno nodded towards me. "Senōr Steele is quite a detective."

"I've been called that," I said. "I also align with your political views. But right now my concern is to find Kon."

He frowned. "If the police have him, that won't be easy."

"I wouldn't expect it. We'll just have to see what we can do. Please tell me what you were doing the other night and what happened afterwards? How did you get away?"

He grinned. "I ran like hell and hid in the bushes."

"It was that easy?"

"Those troopers weren't the sharpest knives in the drawer."

"Why were they were looking for you?"

"It's a long story. "

"But why that night particularly? How did they know you would be there?"

"I don't know. There's an informant, and he or she must be someone close to me. It's worrying."

"Pedro Macias thinks you have an undeclared political rival."

"He's right. And I know who it is."

"An agent of Raul Castro's security forces?"

He shook his head. "Not exactly. There's someone else, a man called Hector Cruz. He is very ambitious politically. He's also dangerous because he holds a senior position in the police force. That's how he can mount the kind of attack he did, the other night."

"What's his agenda?"

"He wants to succeed Raul as president, of course. Like me, he has financial connections in the United States, but his motives are very different. Cruz has struck a Faustian bargain with a Casino owner in Las Vegas. In exchange for funding his career, he has promised to reintroduce gambling if he attains office."

"Is that a good idea?"

"It's a dreadful idea. It would open the door to a flood of crimes – prostitution, drugs, loan sharking, all the sleazy vices that disfigured life under Batista. At least with Fidel we had none of that."

"You sound like a Castro fan."

He grimaced. "Not I. But it's complicated. To many working class Cubans, despite their poverty, Fidel is a hero. On the other hand, look around this fine university. Did you know that public gatherings are forbidden unless they are government spon-sored? It's a kind of Orwellian craziness. Even in retirement Fidel is a monster."

"A dictator, but does that make him a monster?" I

asked. "There have been benevolent dictators in history."

"Oh he's responsible for so many deaths." He smiled sadly. "Some day I will tell you."

I changed the subject. "Tell me about Hector Cruz. How does he operate?"

"He's a senior police officer who has used his position as chief of police for the provinces of Villa Clara and Cienfuegos to build a base, buying the loyalty of several hand-picked lieutenants. I'm convinced that he will launch a putsch just before the next president is installed, whether that be Diáz-Canel or someone else."

"How has he been able to keep all this secret from the authorities?"

Sanchez Madera spread his hands. "The beauty of Cruz's approach is that there's nothing tangible to detect although he operates training camps, barracks and prisons in his territory with military-style discipline."

"How does Raul Castro feel about that?" I asked.

He shrugged. "It's much like Raul's own style. So even if Raul knew, why would he complain?"

"Cruz is hiding his forces in plain sight."

"Exactly."

"Can you prove this?"

Sanchez Madera nodded. "I've complied a thick file on him, based on talking to informants over many months. If published, it would ensure his arrest and possibly his execution."

"He must be desperate to silence you."

"He is. I don't know how he learned that I know about him but, as you saw, I narrowly escaped being sent to his prison island."

I pricked up my ears. "What island?"

"His land-based headquarters are in Cienfuegos on the south coast. But a few kilometres out to sea is the small island of Cayo Piedra."

"And it's a prison?"

"Yes, although it was originally a vacation home for Fidel Castro."

"Really? A good communist like Fidel?"

Sanchez Madera laughed. "Fidel has many homes. Not in his own name perhaps, but when you are the maximum leader that doesn't matter, they are yours."

"And this was his island getaway?"

"That was the plan but it turned out to have disadvantages including a serious mosquito problem so they abandoned the project."

"Abandoned?"

"As Castro's retreat, yes. But scrapping it would have been perceived as an admission of failure. That's something Fidel cannot stand, so there wasn't much opposition when Cruz sought to convert it to other uses."

"When did he start to adapt it as a prison?"

"A couple of years ago. If it's noticed by ordinary citizens, Cruz would say it's a training ground for police recruits, but I have proof that it's a jail, and a most unpleasant one."

"Is that where Kon will be?" I asked.

"Probably, if he's alive."

I stared at him.

"I'm sorry," he said. "One must face facts."

"If he were your friend, how would you rescue him?" I asked.

"From the island? I'd say it was impossible."

"Nothing's impossible," I said. "What would it take?"

Sanchez Madera shrugged. "There is a garrison on the island."

"How large?"

"Eight or ten soldiers. I think it would need a coordinated attack to overcome them." He paused. "Are you serious about this?"

"Yes, I am."

"It will take major resources."

"It will take money," I said.

"Do you have money?"

I thought about Carlton Tisch.

"I might have."

Sanchez Madera shook his head as if in disbelief.

"Well, good luck. I'd like to help but I don't see how I can."

"I have a question," I said. "Aren't you afraid that Cruz will come to your home or the University and arrest you?"

"Unlikely. He wouldn't be able to justify that. Remember, his ambitions are not approved by the State, they are personal to him. If I were in a province within his jurisdiction he could give the order and I would be toast as they say, but I keep well away from his territory. Here in Havana I am safe."

We parted company and I returned to my hotel.

18

"WHAT ARE YOU DOING?" I asked Tisch.

I uttered a quick prayer that the phone was not bugged. I was back in my hotel room, trying to make sense of the problem. Sanchez Madera seemed a decent person, his heart in the right place and not disposed to violence. He had given me plenty to think about and the outline of a plan was starting to form in my mind.

On the face of it, to invade a Cuban island was a completely outrageous idea with international consequences. But on closer inspection I thought it could work under certain conditions.

"Hi," said Carlton. "I was about to jump in the jeep and run down to the marina. Guinevere's bottom needs scraping." Guinevere was the yacht in which he had won Tortola's 'Round the Island' race for seniors three years in a row.

"That may have to wait."

"Why?"

"Remember what Pedro Macias said – or didn't say – about troops training in the Everglades?"

"What of it?"

"I think that's what we're going to need."

I laid it out. I told Carlton that he should contact Pedro Macias. He should also procure a helicopter with enough range for a four hour round trip carrying an assault corps of Macias' commandos. Oh, and make a major transfer of funds, all within forty-eight hours.

I paused for breath. "That's the plan."

"You know," said Carlton, "when you raised the idea it sounded crazy and impossible."

"And now?"

"It's still crazy. But not impossible."

"What's the hardest part?"

"The timing. Getting it all together in two days will be a challenge."

"What about the money?"

"That's no problem. I can wire funds wherever Pedro wants them."

"And the troops?"

"From what Pedro said, that's doable too. His

young men will welcome real action as a change from taking pot-shots at alligators."

"Anything else?"

"I don't know how readily available helicopters are," he mused.

"Make some calls," I said. "I have stuff to do. I'll phone you in a few hours."

My next call was to Bruno.

"This guy Sinbad."

"Yeah?"

"What's he like?"

"He's a good hand."

"What shape is his boat in?"

"So so."

"Would it make it to Cayo Piedra?"

"With Sinbad on board, yes. He understands its engine, problems and all, and he's a good mechanic. Without him, no way."

"Would he be up for something that dangerous?"

"For a price."

19

AFTER LEAVING THE CAMPUS, Martin Sanchez Madera stopped on La Rampa to have his shoes polished.

"*Hola* Señor Martin!" Caleb nodded at Martin who was one of his regulars.

There was no logical reason why Martin should pay to have his shoes shone once a week. Lord knew he had no money to spare, but he did it anyway. It served two purposes, one acknowledged, the other not. First, it was a way of giving something back to those who had even less than he. A handful of non-convertible Cuban pesos, the coins tourists seldom saw, meant more to the recipient than it did to Martin.

But also the act of giving made Martin feel virtuous. There was selfishness about that, if he was honest. He did it as much for himself as for the recipient. Sometimes that thought would flit through his mind and he had enough sense of humour to admit it ruefully. Here he was, holding out to be a socialist but thinking and behaving like a capitalist, dispensing largesse and feeling smug about it.

Caleb was always at his post. The grizzled Cuban looked nearer eighty than seventy, his face lined and dark brown, either from natural pigment or the constant aggression of sun and wind. His station was in a patch of shade in the corner of a small square. A block away were several expensive hotels. More tourists than Cubans had their shoes shined and tourists tipped much more than Cubans but Caleb was still better disposed towards his compatriots and usually had a friendly word and sometimes a tune, for he loved to sing.

"*Hola* Caleb."

They chatted idly.

The two had a musical bond. Caleb had been a fine tenor in his day, performing at social functions and private gatherings. Martin was a fan of *son* and Afro-Cuban jazz and a decent pianist who liked to play jazz keyboard among friends. Caleb had not sung professionally for the simple reason that, early in the Communist regime, the president of the day had closed all nightclubs and casinos, deeming them disgraceful Yankee blemishes on society. That president only lasted seven months, then had differences with Fidel Castro and fled to Miami but by then the damage was done.

Caleb gave a final buffing to Martin's shoes which truth to tell were clean enough already. Martin handed him a few coins which the singer acknowledged with a nod, and went on his way.

20

CARLTON TISCH CALLED Pedro Macias in Hialeah.

"I just heard from Oliver Steele."

"A nice fellow, I liked him."

"He's in Havana. He has a message for you. He wants to know if you can provide a squad of men and a helicopter in two days' time?"

Long pause. "For what?"

"At the moment that is 'need to know' only. But here's a tip: look for Cayo Piedra on the map of Cuba."

Pedro thought rapidly. Then, "It will be expensive."

"I'll pay."

"I'll get back to you."

"When?"

"Tomorrow."

Carlton's phone rang early next morning.

"I'll pick you up in half an hour. We'll take a tour."

Tisch had reluctantly returned to Miami rather than staying on Tortola. He was in a suite at the Omni. A room would have done perfectly well since Mimi was not with him, but Tisch's modus operandi was always to get the biggest and most expensive of everything.

"Where to?"

"Classified. Let's just say that you are going to meet some of my colleagues."

"Okay, I guess."

"Wear casual clothes. We'll be scrambling around and you may get dirty."

Pedro arrived in a Toyota Land Cruiser. It had four wheel drive and Tisch commented on the fact.

Pedro grinned. "We're going to need it."

They drove west out of Miami along the Tamiami Trail which cuts straight across the Everglades before curving at the west coast and heading north towards Tampa.

Halfway across the Everglades, Pedro slowed as

he approached a narrow, unmarked exit. It looked as if it led nowhere but Pedro drove onto it and soon they were bumping over a dirt road into thick vegetation. The trees closed together above their heads to form a canopy and sunshine filtered in, etching dappled patterns on the ground. The road grew narrower, dipping now and then into muddy puddles. The Toyota dealt easily with conditions that would have stranded a conventional car and Tisch understood the reason for the four wheel drive.

The trail forked several times but Pedro seemed to know exactly where he was going. After a while the track petered out completely and the Toyota drew to a halt.

They sat and waited.

"Are we lost?" asked Tisch.

Pedro shook his head.

"So now what?"

"Wait and see." Pedro wound down his window and forest sounds flooded into the cabin, the clicking of crickets, soft rustling of branches and an occasional bird call.

"Are there mosquitos?" Tisch enquired.

"Good point," said Pedro. He reached in the glove box and found a tube of insect repellent. "Rub it on."

Tisch did as he was told and handed the tube back to Pedro who put it away.

"Aren't you going to use any?"

Pedro laughed. "They leave me alone now. They're used to seeing me or perhaps the Cuban meat doesn't taste so good."

A moment later there was movement in the bushes and a figure appeared, a swarthy, broad-shouldered young man in his twenties, deeply tanned. Wearing dark green fatigues and cap, he was almost unnoticeable but he grinned at Pedro.

"Good morning, *Jefe*!"

"Good morning, Luis. This is our friend and colleague, Carlton Tisch."

Luis's nodded politely. "Welcome, Mr. Carlton."

Pedro said, "Luis is a commander in what we call the CLB, the Cuban Liberation Brigade. He will give us the nickel tour."

"From here we go on foot," said Luis, ushering the visitors through a gap in the undergrowth.

"Are you going to leave the Toyota unattended?" Tisch asked.

Pedro laughed. "I don't think many people will be hiking through the jungle today."

Luis smiled. "Bring the keys just in case."

After what seemed like a hundred yards of dense vegetation but was probably only half that, they came to a circular clearing about forty yards across.

Around the perimeter were several tents. There was a cache of firewood piled under a waterproof tarpaulin and a quantity of fuel drums situated well away from the tents. Across the clearing were the outlines of a shed and a wall, although they seemed to be made only of plywood and chicken wire. Tisch wondered what they were for.

In the middle of the clearing stood a helicopter.

"I'm impressed," said Carlton. "You didn't waste any time."

Pedro nodded. "You deserve some of the credit for that. It's much easier to get quick service when one has cash."

"Where did it come from?"

Luis shrugged. "A dealer. He happens to be Hispanic and sympathetic to the idea of a free Cuba. But the fact is, machines like this are available at a price. He also supplied the pilot, Bert, real name Roberto – whose family is Cuban on both sides."

"Is it military surplus?"

"Yes. It's a Sikorsky S-61R, known affectionately as the Jolly Green Giant. It has a capacity of twelve passengers – or eight in full battle gear – plus the pilot. This model went out of production in the 1970's."

"Forty years old? Are you sure it's mechanically sound?"

"I'm not worried about that. The Green Giant has proved hardy and popular over the years. It may be old but it's reliable."

"What about range?"

"This particular version has a range of 780 miles, cruising at 150 miles an hour."

"Is that enough?"

Pedro nodded. "From here to Cayo Piedra is 220 miles as the crow flies but that crow would be over-flying the Cuban mainland which is not a good idea. Cuba's air defence is sophisticated and we would be shot out of the sky, or at least forced to land."

"Which would be embarrassing," said Tisch.

Luis, who was listening, spat in the dust. "For me and my friends it would be worse. Quite likely fatal. The Cuban in the street may be friendly to the U.S. but there's no sympathy at government level for so-called 'enemies of the Revolution.'"

Pedro nodded. "So these young men, my *brigadistas* who are risking their lives, will take a longer route – round the western end of the main-land and then back east. Total distance, close to 700 miles."

"Doesn't leave much room for error," said Tisch.

"No it doesn't. But you know what? If things do go wrong then, between the physical and the polit-ical consequences, we'll all be screwed."

Luis laughed. "Let's think positive. Would you like a demonstration?"

"By all means."

Luis put two fingers in his mouth and whistled.

Half a dozen fatigue-clad figures emerged from the khaki tents, looking much like Luis. Despite the heat they wore body armour and helmets and were armed with pistols and semi-automatic rifles. None of them looked older than thirty. A more senior figure in civilian clothes, stouter and with a big handlebar moustache, trotted alongside them.

"That's Bert, the pilot," explained Pedro.

On the breast pocket of each young commando was a black cloth badge in the shape of an eagle. Pedro saw Carlton looking at it. "That's a reference to *Águila Negra*, Black Eagle, which was a secret code used by the brigade members of the 1961 Bay of Pigs invasion. That exercise was a disaster for many reasons including lax security and bad planning by the C.I.A., with disastrous consequences for the invaders."

"But you plan to do better?"

"I hope so," said Pedro quietly.

Luis joined them and at his signal they boarded the helicopter. It lifted off moments later and rose several hundred feet, rotors throbbing, before disappearing over the tops of the trees. As Tisch and the others watched, the engine noise faded until it could barely be heard.

"What happens now?" asked Tisch.

"Wait and see," said Pedro.

The helicopter's engines grew louder again shortly, and it reappeared. It settled slowly down in the clearing, its skids biting the leaf-strewn earth. Clouds of dust and dirt, stirred up by the rotors, swirled around Tisch and the others. Tisch covered his nose and eyes.

The troopers leaped from the helicopter's open door and sprinted towards the wooden structure that Tisch had noticed when he arrived. A few yards short of it, each man dropped on one knee, took aim and fired.

There was no real gunfire, just a muted popping. The structure, flimsy as it was, did not fall. Instead, large patches of red, blue and yellow appeared as if by magic, making it look for all the world like something in a video game. Their target successfully hit, the troops turned and ran back to the helicopter and all except for Luis leaped on board. Once again the chopper rose above the trees and disappeared.

Luis walked over to the onlookers. "That's what could happen on Cayo Piedra."

"Or something similar," prompted Pedro.

Luis nodded. "Of course. We don't know precisely how things will turn out. Few battle plans survive the first gunfire. But my guys are young and resourceful, they'll be ready for whatever comes."

"How soon can you go?" asked Tisch.

"Tomorrow night if necessary. The weather would be on our side, with very little moon, so conditions will be as good as we can hope for."

"But you'll use live ammunition?"

"Of course," said Pedro. No paint guns on the night."

21

Commander Hector Cruz first met the young woman a year earlier. He saw her walking to work and offered her a ride.

"What's your name?" he asked.

She smiled and blushed. "Teresita."

She shivered in the chill as she climbed into the air-conditioned Mercedes wearing only a thin skirt and blouse. Her dress was chosen for the cigar factory where she worked, sitting at a wooden bench with seventy others and rolling cigars. She was expected to roll a hundred cigars a day or, if working on tightly-rolled expensive brands, slightly less. There was no air conditioning, even in midsummer.

"Do you enjoy your work?" he asked

Sitting in the back beside the smartly uniformed policeman, the girl felt intimidated.

"It's okay." Her fellow workers were friendly enough although she disliked her supervisor, a bullying woman with a loud voice.

Cruz set her down a block away from the factory and watched her walk. He admired the sensuous swing of her hips but what captivated him most was her youth – she could not be more than eighteen.

Knowing that she took the same route every morning, he began to arrange his schedule so as to pick her up.

"When do you get off?" he asked her one day.

"Five o'clock."

"That's a long day."

"It passes quite quickly."

"How do you handle the boredom?"

"They read to us. Newspapers for the men. For the women, romance novels."

The next evening, the Mercedes was waiting round the corner and she got in without a word. When he was still a block away from his house, he stopped the car.

"You had better get down," he smiled. No explanation was necessary.

Soon after their first meeting, he took her to his office and made love to her. The following week they went to an apartment he rented at police expense.

It was quiet there and they would spend several hours. At the end of the evening he would take her in the Mercedes to a corner near where she lived and she would walk home.

She did not hide from her family the fact that she was having an affair. She contributed money to the household and her parents accepted it. Times were hard.

As the weeks went by, Cruz came to take the arrangement for granted, regarding it as a simple contract, exchanging cash for services.

For Teresita, on the other hand, it was an adventure. She let herself hope that one day he would make the relationship permanent. She knew he no longer slept with his wife who had been a noted beauty in what passed for Cuban society, the Castros' circle of friends. She had born Cruz three children but had grown tired of his philandering and they occupied separate bedrooms.

So it was a shock when, staring out of the window of the factory one day, Teresita saw his Mercedes cruising slowly down the road. He was in the back but he was not alone. Sitting on his left – *in my place*, she thought – was a woman no older than Teresita herself, laughing and talking. Her smiling face was coffee coloured and her lipstick scarlet.

There was something about her animated, over-the-top manner that set Teresita's teeth on edge. She could not understand why Cruz would drive by her workplace until she realised he had probably never seen the factory. He certainly seemed unaware of his surroundings as he listened to the woman, a cold smile on his pale face, one hand stroking his pointed beard.

She spent the rest of the shift in a daze.

"Penny for your thoughts!" said her neighbour, a young black called Felipe.

"Excuse me?"

"You were a million miles away. You'll never make your quota at that rate."

She laughed without humour. "As if I cared."

"Anything I can help with?"

She shook her head.

When the time came to leave work, she started to walk home but the Mercedes appeared as usual and stopped to pick her up. She behaved as if nothing untoward had happened.

Back at the apartment, Cruz was more than usually amorous. Despite herself, Teresita too felt stimulated and their lovemaking was strenuous. As they lay exhausted afterwards she said, "I saw you this afternoon."

"What do you mean?"

"In your car. You drove past the factory. I was looking out of the window and I saw you."

She was watching him and his manner told the tale – his face went still. He was obviously taken by surprise.

"I forgot that was where you worked. It was a busy day and I was pursuing a case." His eyes met hers, then shifted away.

"There was a woman in the car," she said.

She could sense the cogs clicking and whirring in his brain.

"Yes. She's a witness. We are close to nailing a black market ring and she's an informant."

It was a weak excuse. It was unlikely a policeman of his rank would spend his time pursuing black marketeers. The black market was an integral part of the economy with customers everywhere.

"She's very pretty," said Teresita.

Cruz shrugged. "I guess so."

He changed the subject. Their relationship continued, apparently unchanged, but the more Teresita thought about it the more she came to despise herself for giving in to him. The money only made things worse. She couldn't help seeing herself as just a prostitute.

From then on, she was determined to bring him down.

22

———

"You wanted an update," said the gaoler Marco. He was phoning Cruz from Cayo Piedra. "He's been in the *caja* for eighteen hours."

"Any progress?"

"No. When we opened the lid he was unconscious. He came to and looked at us."

"Did he say anything?"

"It was hard to make out but I think he said 'Go to hell.'"

Cruz tried to feel calm but it was not easy.

There was a skeleton in his past, a crucial mistake he had made, and unfortunately Martin Sanchez Madera knew about it. Now, that fact could blow Cruz's plans sky high.

Cruz had realised early on that he needed to raise money. His first effort to do so involved collaborating with Igor Kirov, manager of purchase accounting at the Russian embassy.

The two of them had set up a scam involving bogus invoices. Whenever Cruz needed parts for his police force's aging vehicles – all of which were Russian – he would send Igor a purchase order. He would also approve payment of an inflated amount and he and Igor would split the difference. The arrangement had made them both rich.

But recently the scheme had been exposed. A young auditor named Pavel, examining Igor's department, had discovered the scam.

By sheer coincidence, auditor Pavel and Martin Sanchez Madera were neighbours and the two men had become friendly. Over a beer, Pavel had shared his audit problem, explaining that he had confronted Igor with his findings giving him the chance to rebut.

Igor, in a panic, had gone straight to Cruz.

Cruz believed in swift action. The auditor must be neutralised. Cruz couldn't arrest him, but there were other ways. Two nights later as Pavel was walking home in the dark, a car mounted the pavement, hit him and carried him for several yards. His crumpled body was left on the side of the road.

The morning after Pavel's death, Igor's phone

rang. It was Cruz. "Pavel won't be bothering us. But I have a question."

"Yes?" Igor tried to sound cool.

"Who else knew about this?"

"In this building, nobody."

"What about outside?"

"I never discuss my work outside the office."

"What about your wife?"

"I'm not married." But a thought struck Igor. "The auditor was friends with a university professor, a man called Martin Sanchez Madera. They drank together."

"What are you saying?"

"I hope Pavel didn't mention that particular audit to Sanchez Madera."

There was a long pause.

"I see," said Cruz.

Over the next few days, he thought about the situation. He saw two needs.

First, he must silence Sanchez Madera before the academic exposed Cruz as crook, or a rival to the Castros, or both. Cruz knew what happened to Castro's rivals. They ended up in prison or dead. For instance, Fidel arrested his fellow freedom fighter Uber Matos and imprisoned him for twenty years. Che Guevara went abroad after the revolution but was shot leading an insurrection in Bolivia. Camilo Cienfuegos, who matched or even exceeded Fidel in popularity, was killed in a mysterious 'plane crash. More recently, two foreign ministers – Felipe Perez Roque and Roberto Robaina – and Carlos Lage Dávila, a former de facto prime minister of Cuba, rose to senior positions but were demoted or dismissed. Cruz couldn't risk ending up the same way which was odds on to happen if Sanchez Madera spread the word.

Second, with the Russian money dried up, he must find another source of funds. One place to look was overseas. The exile community in Florida perhaps? He put out feelers. Someone suggested Miguel de la Paz, a wealthy businessman. Since leaving Cuba, De La Paz had built a successful construction company and had a handsome home in Orlando.

Cruz spoke to him via Skype.

"Why do you need money?" de la Paz asked pleasantly.

Cruz launched into a prepared speech saying he would inspire the counter revolution that he was sure de la Paz desired.

"What will I get in return?" de la Paz the businessman.

"The property that was taken from you by Castro."

Cruz had done his homework. When Castro came to power, along with the vast acreages of the

United Fruit Company and others, the de la Paz ranch in Oriente was confiscated without compensation.

De la Paz laughed. "But I have all the assets I need, my friend. And my life is here in the States now."

Cruz was afraid his appeal had been wasted. Then de la Paz said something that made him think: "You need someone who is more motivated to work with you."

Cruz asked himself, what kind of wealthy American would most appreciate a powerful ally in Cuba?

So he contrived an introduction to Stanley Rothman, founder and owner of the Portofino Casino Group.

23

"VERY IMPRESSIVE," said Stanley Rothman.

He and Cruz had just met for the first time in the lobby of the Hotel Nacional.

He indicated the huge portrait of Fidel that dominated the lobby. It was the picture, said to be Fidel's favourite, of a virile black bearded soldier in fatigues, with rifle and backpack.

Cruz nodded. "El Comandante. A fine man and an inspiration to us all."

Rothman glanced sharply at Cruz. Was he being ironic? But Cruz's face was impassive, showing only a polite smile of greeting. He was in plain clothes but his suit, like his uniforms, was cut to fit. With his pointed beard, sleek black hair and flashing eyes he could have been an actor or playboy or even a younger, suaver edition of Fidel himself.

Rothman had travelled to Cuba legally on a cultural tour. Such tours had to be in approved form but this was no problem for Rothman since his empire included a licensed travel agency. There were some tiresome conditions including writing a daily journal but for that he was accompanied by a young female secretary, one of whose less colorful jobs was to keep the required records.

Cruz put an arm round Rothman's shoulders and ushered him out onto the patio. They walked across the paved area to the grass beyond and sat down on a wrought iron bench.

"Something to drink?" Cruz beckoned a waiter.

"What do you suggest?"

"A *Mojito*, of course."

"What is that?"

"Rum, lime juice, soda water with fresh mint and sugar cane in a tall glass."

"Sounds good."

"It's the spirit of Cuba."

They sipped their drinks. The hotel lawn was elevated, enabling them to look out across the highway to the Malecon, the low walled pedestrian promenade that curved the length of downtown Havana, fronting the ocean.

"Your first visit?" Cruz asked.

Rothman nodded. "But not the last, I hope."

"These are interesting times."

"But maybe difficult."

Cruz smiled. "There are opportunities for businessmen willing to seize them."

"Cuba is still a communist country, is it not?"

"For now. But already thirty percent of the working population are employed in the private sector."

"Foreign ownership of businesses is impossible, isn't it?"

"Yes, but that's why you are here." Cruz leaned forward. "Soon the regime will change."

"You're not talking about overthrowing the Castros?"

"Of course not. God and time will do that. Fidel is ninety and unwell. Raul is eighty-five – he'll step down when his term ends in 2018."

"Who will succeed him?"

Cruz spread his hands wide. "That, my friend, is the question."

The waiter approached and Cruz ordered more *Mojitos*.

Rothman had come prepared. "Here's how I see things. I'm in the casino business. Diáz-Canel, the most likely successor to Raul, is by all accounts an upstanding character who may not permit gambling, a business wrongly associated with crime, prostitution and worse."

"You are correct. But his succession is not

guaranteed."

"Who else could it be?"

"Who do you think?" Their eyes met.

Rothman saw a clean cut, energetic young individual. Good looking, intense and very political. There was an unattractive sourness about him when he smiled, but he had an imposing presence and looked like a man with a future.

Their drinks arrived and Cruz pushed Rothman's glass towards him. From a pocket he produced a cigar in a metal tube and offered it to Rothman. "A cigar?"

Rothman examined the label. "Romeo y Julieta. You have good taste. Even in Cuba these must be expensive."

"I have a source. But let's talk about money. That's where you can help."

"Now we're getting to the point," said Rothman. "How much do you need? What for? And what will I get in return?"

Cruz nodded. "Two million dollars. A tiny fraction of your net worth."

Rothman smiled faintly. "Go on."

"In return, on Day One of my administration, I will approve an application by you for a new casino in Havana."

For the first time since they started talking, both men relaxed.

"Well it took half an hour and a couple of *Mojitos* but I think we have an understanding," said Rothman.

He stood up, looking at his watch. They strolled to the edge of the lawn and gazed out to sea. Between the hotel and the Malecon was a busy divided highway with motor traffic flowing in both directions.

"I see a lot of those fine old cars."

"But also many newer vehicles," Cruz pointed out.

"Changing times." Rothman was expansive.

They walked back through the lobby and out to the front of the hotel. A car drew up and Cruz got in. A new Mercedes, Rothman noted.

It was not until it was out of sight that he realised Cruz had not addressed his second question – how did he plan to use Rothman's money?

24

"I NEED to get to that island," I told Bruno.

We were in the rooftop bar of the Ambos Mundos. The mellow rooftops of Havana made a faded, dusty patchwork that stretched to the sea.

He blinked. "Is that wise, Mr. Oliver? It's a very dangerous place."

"I know, but to hell with it. How can you get me there fast?"

Bruno's open face clouded as he struggled for a polite response. "You would need a boat, obviously."

"I want to meet your friend Sinbad. Where is he?"

"He lives in Caibarién, near Remedios. It is two hundred miles east of here."

"What are we waiting for?"

· · ·

Despite his mohawk hairdo and entrepreneurial bent Bruno was a nervous driver and the van rattled along at a steady fifty miles an hour. It was a pleasant drive though, past sugarcane and tobacco fields and green pasture with cattle grazing.

We stopped after a while at a roadside café. There were a couple of long distance coaches in the parking lot. I found myself surrounded by tourists chatting noisily in English and waving cameras. I wondered if they had any idea of the roiling undercurrents in the shadow of the country they were blithely snapping with their Canons and mobile phones.

Back on the road we finally got to Caibarién. Bruno made straight for the dock. We pulled up by a jetty to which was tethered a nondescript fishing boat.

'Hola," shouted Bruno.

A wiry individual with a weather-beaten face emerged from the cockpit and stared at us. He looked about fifty, with a seaman's gaunt profile, any spare flesh etched away by wind and sun. Recognising Bruno, he nodded with the ghost of a smile.

Bruno shook his hand. "This is a friend from the United States. We need to talk."

Sinbad eyed me appraisingly and beckoned us aboard. I'm no expert but to me the boat looked barely seaworthy. It was also in serious need of cleaning, its wooden planks caked with salt and grime. A small structure served as the wheelhouse. The deck was open, apart from a rusty metal framework supporting a threadbare fabric canopy intended to provide protection from rain and sun. There was room for maybe a dozen passengers but the thought of attempting the perilous crossing to Florida fully loaded made me shudder.

"I need a vessel to get me from Cienfuegos to an island south west of there called Cayo Piedra," I said.

"I know Cayo Piedra."

"Really?"

He looked at me, amused. "I've been sailing these waters a long time. I know all the islands."

"Do you know what goes on there?"

He shrugged. "Of course."

"A friend of mine is on that island and I want to get him off."

His expression did not change but he raised an eyebrow, turned to Bruno and spoke in rapid Spanish. I caught the word *peligro* several times.

Bruno turned to me. "He says it would be tricky. Not the sea journey, that is straightforward, but the mission itself."

"Well, he's right. Does that scare him?"

Sinbad spat over the side.

"No," said Bruno, "but it will cost you."

"How much?" I did not care, it was a necessary expense, but I felt I should bargain.

Sinbad turned to face me. He might not speak much English but he seemed to understand it when he needed to. "A thousand."

I stuck out a hand and he shook it.

"I'll pay you in advance," I said.

He shook his head. "After. If we are both alive."

Bruno said, "His father was imprisoned by Castro many years ago for criticising the regime. An informant overheard him in a bar and he was arrested and sentenced to fifteen years."

"I see. Is his father alive?"

"He died in prison."

25

"WHAT NOW?" asked Bruno as we waved Sinbad on his way and watched him disappear west into the afternoon sun.

"We have to get to Cienfuegos," I said. "I guess we just point south and drive."

Sinbad had agreed to take his boat to Cienfuegos, sailing round the western tip of Cuba and back into southern waters. It would take him thirty-six hours. I could have asked Bruno to find us a different boat somewhere on the south coast but I was impressed with Sinbad. I liked his stoic attitude and, based on our brief exchanges, I felt I could trust him. Besides, it would take a while for the other arm of our attack – by air – to be ready, so the timing worked.

I did not share my plans for an airborne attack with either Bruno or Sinbad. At the back of my mind was the risk of one of them being captured and if they didn't know my plans they couldn't give them away.

Bruno nodded. "We can stop overnight in Santa Clara. It is a medium sized town, the capital of Villa Clara province. I know a hotel with decent wifi and phone service that you can use if you need to."

"Good." I was starting to feel progress. There was no telling how Kon was, or even if he was still alive but I was doing my best. It was all I could do.

Half an hour later Bruno pulled off the road and stopped by a green space, surrounding some kind of memorial.

"Is this Santa Clara?"

"It is the outskirts. I want to show you something."

We got out and I looked around. Across the green was an old railroad car and, opposite, a bulldozer on a concrete plinth.

"This is a monument to a key battle in the revolution," said Bruno. "It was Che Guevara's greatest victory. In December 1958, with only 300 men, he conquered the city which was defended by 3,000 of Batista's soldiers."

"Why the bulldozer?"

"He derailed a train carrying government troops and weapons. That's the bulldozer that was used to break up the track and cause the derailment."

"Che seems to have been a genuine hero."

Bruno shrugged. "His heroic status is secure because he is dead. Had he lived, and stayed in Cuba, who knows if the island would have been big enough for Fidel and Che to share?"

"What do you mean?"

"So many heroes of the revolution died or were imprisoned. General Ochoa was executed for 'betraying the trust of the people of Cuba.' Huber Matos was imprisoned for many years. Jose Abrantés, a former Minister of the Interior was sentenced to twenty years in 1989 and died in prison two years later. Only Fidel's brother Raul has stayed the course."

"What are you saying? Fidel would have been paranoid to make all those things happen."

"Paranoid? Perhaps you should ask his personal bodyguard Juan Sánchez who was imprisoned just because he told Fidel he wanted to resign."

"What happened to him?"

"He defended himself vigorously in court but served several years in prison, then fled to Miami where he wrote a bestselling book. At least he escaped, unlike many – he died in Florida in 2013."

We drove into Santa Clara. There was a pleasant

leafy square with a bandstand and a statue of Leoncio Vidal, hero of the 1895 War. It was hard not to think of Cuba as a country forged in blood. It seemed peaceful now thanks to the strict regime, but with Fidel retired and Raul getting ready to step down how long would that peace last?

We parked in a side street off the main square. Carrying our bags we approached a well kept building whose sign proclaimed it as the Magnolia Guest House. Bruno ushered me inside. "This should do for us."

I looked around. Everything was clean and a light breeze freshened the air in the small lobby. "It looks fine."

Across the street a man in his forties wearing a white guayabera shirt and dark slacks watched Oliver and Bruno get out of the van. He pulled a scrap of paper from his pocket and read a number scrawled on it, comparing it with the license plate on the van. Satisfied that they were the same, he took out his mobile 'phone and tapped a number on speed-dial. It took him straight to Hector Cruz in his office in Cienfuegos.

The man spoke briefly, reporting where he was and what he had seen. Cruz listened and gave him brief instructions.

After that, the man strolled over to the guest house. He presented a card of identification to the clerk behind the desk. She looked at it and called the manager who appeared promptly. Words were exchanged. Then the two disappeared into the manager's office and the door closed behind them.

26

I CONNECTED my computer to the power outlet in my room in the guest house and read my email. There was a message from Tisch. I had asked him to keep me posted, but to be circumspect. The message read:

"Hope you're enjoying your well-earned vacation.

"Am assembling equipment for the Everglades project. I've located a vehicle. It is large and has the necessary range given the lack of gas stations on our route.

"Our subcontractor's staff are undergoing special training in order to minimise industrial accidents. We're determined to maintain our fine safety record.

"Subcontractor has asked for site maps. Can you supply?

I approved. It was nice and bland. I didn't know whether emails could be hacked in Cuba but I wanted to take no chances. I had to smile at those in the U.S. who had doubted if wifi was available in Cuba. True, I had only been in decent hotels but so far I had been able to pick it up perfectly.

The last paragraph made me scratch my head. Of course Pedro and his brigade would need maps but where on earth was I going to get them?

The only source I could think of was Martin Sanchez Madera and I did not have contact details for him. Then I remembered Bruno had done business with him and should have his phone number.

His room was across the corridor. I knocked and opened the door. There was an open bottle of rum on the desk and Bruno was drinking rum and cola from a tooth mug. He had had a couple already.

"Sure" he said expansively when I asked for Sanchez Madera's number. Before I could stop him, he picked up the hotel phone and dialled the number. I heard an answering voice on the line and he handed me the receiver with a flourish.

"Martin, it's Oliver Steele. I know this is a long shot but do you have a map of Cayo Piedra? We need to know the layout, understand what we're getting into."

"No, but I know where you can get one."

"We need it soonest. I'm in Santa Clara. I don't know how good the stores are here, it's not the United States or even Havana."

Martin laughed. "I'll make it easy for you. Does your hotel have wifi?"

"Yes, there's a good signal."

"I'm going to give you the coordinates of the island relative to Cienfuegos, okay?

"Okay."

"From the centre of Cienfuegos, go twenty-four kilometres due south. Then turn and go sixty-four kilometres east. Have you got that?"

I grabbed a pencil and jotted it down. "What do I do with it?"

"Open Google Maps, choose Satellite View and there you are."

I couldn't help laughing. "That simple?"

"Yep. Anything else?"

"Not right now. Have a good evening."

"Thanks. My wife has prepared *ropa vieja* with rice, beans and fried plantains, a classic Cuban meal."

"You've earned it."

It was easy to bring up an image of the island. I zoomed in until the picture started to lose focus and Bruno and I studied it.

We could see buildings at the north, or narrow end. From their rectangular layout I guessed they were the cell blocks. We could even make out a high fence around the prison compound which was set at the northern tip of the island with the terrain outside falling away sharply to the sea. Further north still there was a second, smaller island, apparently deserted and connected by a long bridge or causeway.

South of the compound was an office building and beyond that a clearing which looked large enough for a helicopter to land. Farther south was what looked like a barracks.

"This is perfect," Bruno crowed. "All we need now is a printer."

"We don't even need that, " I said. "I just need to get the coordinates to Pedro and he can print it at his end. Then they can practise manoeuvres until they have it perfect."

I decided, on second thoughts, to give the information to Carlton Tisch instead and let him forward it to Pedro. I called the Tortola villa. Mimi answered.

"He's in his den, I'll buzz him." Carlton had a studio in a separate wing of the cliff-side villa a few feet up the hill where he would retreat when he didn't want to be disturbed.

"Kathy's here, by the way."

"What are you folk up to?"

"Not much. Played some tennis. Had a swim."

Carlton had built an infinity pool by excavating a massive hole in the rock below the terrace. You could float, gazing out across the Caribbean in perfect tranquillity. "Hang on," said Mimi, "Here he is."

"What?" barked Tisch.

"Write this down," I said. You have to be brusque with Carlton. If you're polite he thinks you're a sissy. A Wall Street thing?

"Got it. Now what?"

"Phone it through to Pedro. He can open up Google Earth and print the map, then have his commandos refine their plan of attack."

"What are your own plans?"

"I've arranged a boat. While the helicopter is touching down Bruno and I will approach by sea, sneak in and spirit Kon away. Or something."

It was only when he asked that I realised I hadn't figured out just how to make it all work. Carlton's questions often have that effect. He is annoying, but helpful.

"Just be careful," he said.

"Will do. Is Kathy around?"

"She's here somewhere."

"Put her on."

I heard her voice. "Where are you?"

"In a hotel in central Cuba."

"Are you okay?"

"Never better. I'm about to invade an island full of heavily armed guards, not sure exactly whose – Castro's or somebody's."

I try not to be facetious at key moments but remarks like that just slip out.

"I'm thinking of you," she said.

"Likewise."

"Do you need any help?"

"With the invasion? How?"

"Maybe as backup or liaison, stuff like that," she said.

"How would you do that?"

I don't know but most good armies have it."

"Have what?"

'Backup and liaison."

"I'll be fine," I said. The conversation was heading in a tricky direction.

"Okay my love," she said sweetly.

"Glad we got that clear."

"Fine. Love you!"

"Love you too!" I said.

I had an early start next morning so I went to bed.

In the hotel manager's office, the guayabera man was studying a printout of the calls from Oliver's room. He couldn't make much sense of the overseas calls but the one Bruno made to Havana was another matter. The guayabera man phoned the number through to Cruz immediately.

27

BRUNO, despite his friendly open manner, had been less than frank with Oliver about his involvement with Sanchez Madera, when he said he only knew him as Martin.

In fact, he had known the academic for some time and had even introduced him to Teresita from the cigar factory.

A year ago, out of the blue, Teresita had phoned him. "I hear you buy cigars."

"Sometimes."

"I work in the Tabacuba factory."

Bruno knew immediately what she wanted. As a state employee, Teresita only earned $25 a month, but her work in the cigar factory came with a valuable perk: she was allowed to take home an occasional cigar. Cigars varied in quality depending on the leaf and how tightly it was rolled. The cheapest cost a few cents, the most expensive, fifty dollars or more. Whether the difference in smoking pleasure justified such a big mark-up could be debated but there was a market for even the most expensive and Bruno knew where to find it.

"I pay five dollars for a full sized Partagas or Romeo y Julieta," he said.

She felt she should negotiate. "They retail for much more."

"I know, but I have expenses and I need to make a profit. Anyway, that's the going rate – you can ask your friends."

She had already done so. "How many can you take?"

"As many as they let you have. If you get even more, we can talk."

That would require her to steal which some might try but not Teresita, she hadn't the nerve. It was difficult anyway under the watchful eye of the manageress and was punishable by dismissal.

So they reached agreement. For Teresita, the extra money was crucial.

She visited Bruno regularly to hand over the product and they became friendly. Both were young and good looking but he never made a pass at her.

She sometimes wondered if he was gay. But he was easy to talk to and she enjoyed her trips to the city.

They were chatting one day. It had been a while since her last trip.

"My situation has changed," she said.

He raised an eyebrow. "Really?"

"I have income from another source now."

"None of my business," he laughed.

It was the right thing to say if he wanted her to confide. She smiled drily. "I'm having a sordid affair with a married man."

She mentioned that the individual was highly ranked in the police force. She did not say his name, but she hinted he had political ambitions and at this Bruno's antennae snapped to attention.

A few months later, when he began to sense that all was not well between Teresita and her lover, he thought about connecting her with Martin. As a market trader, Bruno sympathised with Martin's politics. Trade had made him prosperous and impatient of the system of government. He didn't know exactly what Martin was up to politically but he was inclined to give him a helping hand, so he put him in touch with Teresita.

Martin wasted no time in getting to know the young woman and she soon became a regular reporter of pillow talk from Hector Cruz. She even mentioned his illegal arrangement with the Russian embassy. With what Martin learned from her and from the auditor Pavel, he was able to put together a solid case against the corrupt policeman.

28

AFTER LEAVING Oliver and Bruno at the University, Martin's next destination was the Memories Hotel in Miramar, where he had an appointment to play squash.

Ten minutes later, changed and ready, he shook hands with one Dr. Sandy Clark from the United States, who was in Havana for a medical conference.

Martin was the younger man and faster around the court but he had trouble dealing with his opponent's wily drop shots and subtle variations in pace and they split six close games.

Clark explained afterwards that he was pleasantly surprised to find squash courts, and players, in Havana.

Martin smiled ruefully. "We're a very small group. As far as I know this is the only hotel in

Havana with a court and in the rest of Cuba I know of nothing."

"How did you get involved in the game?"

"My grandfather played at Yale many years ago, before Castro came to power. When I was small he taught me the rudiments, hitting against the wall in a fronton, the court where jai alai is played. That wasn't real squash of course but I always wanted to play properly so when this hotel built its courts I got in touch with them. Now, when visitors like you are looking for a game, they call me. How long are you staying in Havana?"

"After this, for a change of scenery, I shall be spending a few days at a hotel on Cayo Santa Maria."

"No squash in that part of the country I'm afraid. But you might want to take a look at *frontenis*, a game played in a fronton with something like a tennis racquet. That's probably the closest thing."

With Clark promising to think about it, they parted and Martin went home.

That evening at his home in Havana, he sighed. "Duty calls."

He frowned and picked up a pile of essays submitted by his class, which he needed to read before the morning.

He had just finished supper and helped his wife Sylvia clear the dishes in their small flat in the Miramar district. Sylvia had washed them in the kitchen sink – a dishwasher was out of the question on Martin's government salary. Now she was getting ready to visit her sister who was married to a physician at the nearby hospital and lived a few blocks away.

There was a loud knock at the door and she answered it.

Two men stood there. One wore police uniform, the grey shirt and blue trousers of the PNR. The other was in plain clothes.

"Your husband, please."

"Just a moment." She turned to fetch him but Martin had already come to the door.

"Martin Sanchez Madera?"

"That's me."

The man in plain clothes smiled politely. "We must ask you to come with us."

"May I ask why?"

"Nothing grave. You may be able to help us with some enquiries we are making."

Sanchez Madera was not so naive as to misunderstand the request. He had known for several years that, despite all his precautions, he might be arrested at any time.

He forced himself to appear natural. "If I can

help the State in any way. May I ask the subject of your enquiries?"

The plainclothes detective's smile did not waver. "They are general."

Sanchez Madera shrugged. "I'll fetch my coat."

The uniformed policeman stepped forward and grasped him by the arm. "It's not necessary."

Sylvia moved forward anxiously but Sanchez Madera waved her away.

"This shouldn't take long. It's all right, go visit your sister."

"I love you," she said, her voice shaking. Questions raced through her mind, all of them frightening, but she could only stand at the door and watch in silence as he was ushered down the concrete stairs and into an unmarked car.

He sat in the back of the car next to the plain clothes detective. The uniformed policeman drove. There was a click as he locked all four doors from a control on the dash.

"Where are we going?" Sanchez Madera asked.

The detective shook his head. "Not far."

"I've done nothing wrong."

"Then you have nothing to worry about."

"I'd still like to know where we're going."

"I'm just doing my job, my friend." Not smiling now.

Sanchez Madera suspected the man was simply not senior enough to know the details of the case.

At the local police station he was led inside and put in a plain interrogation room with a table and a couple of chairs. The room was heavily air conditioned, he suspected on purpose, and he was uncomfortably cold in his thin shirt.

He was left alone for half an hour. He paced to and fro to keep warm. Finally, the door opened and a different man came in. He wore a sweater and carried a manila folder.

"Sit," the man said. He consulted his folder. "You had a phone call today from a hotel in Santa Clara."

The statement invited a reply but Sanchez Madera said nothing. The man rapped the table. "Yes?"

Martin's mind raced. Things were bad. It was beyond trying to pretend ignorance. The police must know of the connection between him and Kon's aborted boat trip from Matanzas. But there must be more going on. There would not have been all this fuss over an ordinary citizen fleeing Cuba. People tried to leave all the time and many were caught. Usually they were fined, a slap on the wrist. But someone somewhere knew he was not a simple case.

He was not just – what was the American term? – an economic refugee.

His main feeling was of anger directed at himself. He had miscalculated badly. He had believed that as long as he stayed out of the provinces of Cienfuegos and Villa Clara, Hector Cruz's area of authority, he was safe.

He sighed. "What of it? A visitor from the United States, who I met by chance, is touring the country. I don't know why he's in Santa Clara but it's a pleasant town. The Guevara monument is there, and other attractions."

"What did you talk about?"

"Tourism. Places of interest. I said he should visit Trinidad for its beauty and its history and he said he would try to do so."

The interrogator nodded but he was clearly not buying Martin's story. "Why was this visitor travelling with the same man who drove you to Matanzas the other night?"

So that was it. They would have recorded the license number of Bruno's van. Someone had seen the vehicle in Santa Clara and called it in.

Martin remained quiet. But he had no illusions that silence would save him. He feared the worst. Torture and coercion were common when the authorities wanted to convict a subject and the catchall charge of betraying or tainting the Revolution was all but impossible to refute.

The man stood up and left. Martin shivered. His bladder was bursting. Another twenty minutes went by.

Finally two individuals entered who he had not seen before, both in plain clothes, and led him outside.

"At least let me use the bathroom," he said angrily.

They watched as he stood at the urinal.

"What happens next?" he asked.

One of them shrugged. "You have a long journey ahead."

"I need to phone my wife."

The request was ignored. He was led out to a police van with a different driver. This time he was handcuffed before being shoved in the back.

He could see through the bars of the rear window that they were leaving Havana and heading east. He knew the road well; they seemed to be heading for Santa Clara or possibly Cienfuegos.

Beyond that, the future was uncertain.

CRUZ WAS in his office in Cienfuegos. The phone rang. It was Absequa, his contact in Havana.

"Sanchez Madera is in a prison van and the van is already on the road. We should be with you in a little while."

"Don't bring him here," snapped Cruz. "Take him to the Training Centre, it's more discreet."

He hung up, then drove to the Police Training Centre which was in a compound on the edge of town. Its entrance was set back from the road at the end of a long driveway so it was inconspicuous although it covered many acres. Passers-by usually assumed it was just a farm or did not notice it at all.

The Centre had been set up by Fidel Castro in the 1970's as a place to train insurgents from overseas in the days when Cuba was a breeding ground for world terrorism. Those days were gone now. Fidel was old and frail and Cuba was less active on the world stage. For Cruz the Centre served a different purpose.

He sat in the canteen sipping a beer, pleased about catching this young man, a potential thorn in his side.

There was the sound of a vehicle arriving and shortly a dishevelled Sanchez Madera, his wrists handcuffed behind him, was pushed before Cruz by two guards.

He stood defiantly as Cruz looked him up and down. "What have you got to say for yourself, my friend?"

"What do you mean?"

"I'm told you have a dossier containing some malicious nonsense about me."

Martin Sanchez Madera was a politician but he was above all an intellectual and even when he should have kept silent the urge to debate was irresistible. "Not so."

"What is in it?"

"What if I told you that I have documented the value of Russian automobile equipment delivered to this Centre and others like it?"

"I have no idea what you mean," said Cruz but there was an edge to his voice.

"I compared that with the amounts your department paid for the equipment, which is much greater. What happened to the difference?"

Cruz flushed, then said coldly, "You don't understand how the world works."

"I understand that you're a thief, hardly presidential material, and yet when Raul gives up the Presidency you hope to become president yourself."

"You know that how?"

"Call it an educated guess."

"Well, education won't help you because you won't be around to see it happen."

Sanchez Madera could not resist playing his strongest card. "I've arranged for the file to be delivered directly to Raul Castro's office."

"By whom?"

"By my wife."

Cruz shook his head. He turned to Absequa who had been listening with a smirk on his face. "Take care of that!"

"Yes, Chief." He hurried from the room.

Cruz turned to Sanchez Madera. "Thank you for being so helpful. My men will visit your apartment and clean out every scrap of paper in it. As for your wife . . ." He paused, but the inference was plain.

30

"HEY GRANDPA, want to sell your hat?" an urchin shouted at Caleb in the street. He grinned and shrugged. The kid was right to tease him, he was fair game.

Caleb, the shoeshine man who polished Martin Sanchez Madera's shoes, was a singer. At the age of seventy his voice was not as strong as in his prime but his tempo as he belted out *son* and *bolero* was as on-point as ever. You couldn't listen to him without getting drawn into the rhythm.

He was on his way to the Old Town for an audition. He wasn't sure for what. Someone called Pepe, who sounded young, had called and said something about putting together a new act along the lines of the Buena Vista Social Club, the group that achieved international success following the 1999 documentary by director Wim Wenders. Pepe had asked Caleb to wear stage clothes – jacket and tie and the felt homburg beloved of many Cuban singers.

So he was smartly dressed as he approached the small office off San Francisco Square. He felt ridiculous, such clothes were for the stage and were too formal and too hot for parched Havana streets, but at least they were black, not rainbow or pastel, like some performers.

Inside, a bespectacled young Cuban in shirt sleeves and flashy waistcoat, necktie loosely knotted, nodded at him.

"What's the deal?" asked Caleb. The fellow looked callow, a rapacious owl behind big glasses. *I guess it's the new Cuba*, he thought.

"One of my people heard you sing at some wedding. They thought you might fit with what we're doing."

"Who is 'we,' and what is it you're doing?"

"I'm putting together a group along the lines of the BVSC to tour Canada and Europe. My U.S. partner is financing it."

"Okay," said Caleb. He didn't really understand, but if it meant work, whatever the young man said was fine with him. "Do you want me to sing something?"

"Sure."

Caleb frowned in thought. His lined face was a

map of his life. Born in a poor village in Oriente in 1940, he was eighteen when Fidel stormed Havana and proclaimed the revolution. He had a strong singing voice but the new President Urrutia, a devout Christian, closed the casinos and nightclubs, the sort of places where Caleb might have earned a living.

As a young man he was also a good athlete and had ambitions as a runner, so he hoped instead to achieve distinction on the track. Fidel was anxious for Cuba to excel at the Olympics and other international events. The 1500 meters was Caleb's best distance. He did well at first but he was not quite international standard and when it became clear that he would not reach the heights, the State lost interest in its callous way.

Instead he drifted from one manual job to another and by the time he reached middle age he was reduced to shining shoes for a living. He was not bitter about that, it was life in Cuba, it was how things were.

He smiled. "Whatever I like?"

"Sure," said the young man. He fidgeted. Caleb suspected he was not very musical.

There was a piano in the corner.

"May I?" he asked.

"Be my guest."

He sat at the piano, hitching up his trouser legs

to protect the thin fabric well worn at the knees. He
played a few chords and in a low voice began to sing:

"El carino que te tengo
Yo no lo puedo negar
Se me sale la babita
Yo no lo puedo evitar"

The love that I'm feeling,
Cannot be denied,
I want you all over,
It's something I can't hide.

It was 'Chan Chan,' a favourite of his and he always
felt sentimental when he sang it. He came to the
end, turned and looked at his interviewer in enquiry.

Pepe was unmoved by the beauty of the piece.
"That's a love song. Give me something stronger,
with a beat."

Caleb sighed. He knew what the man meant. He
had stood on many flimsy stages, microphone in
hand, spotlight in his face, dark suit and hat lending
an air of gangster Chicago. The smell of cigar smoke
and cheap rum, scratchy speakers turned up too
loud, defiantly cheerful but tinged with melancholy.
It was stand-up music. He had no microphone but it
was not necessary in the small room. He cleared his

throat, drew breath and launched into *'El cuarto de Tula:'*

"Al cuarto de Tula, le cogió candela.
    Se quedó dormida y no apagó la vela."

Tula's Room caught fire.
    She fell asleep and didn't put out her candle.

He belted out a couple of verses before turning to his interviewer with an ironic bow.

The irony went un-noticed.

"Okay," said Pepe. "We'll let you know." He turned away.

So that was that, thought Caleb. No luck this time. But he was not devastated, there had been many disappointments, one more unsuccessful audition didn't mean much. He would just go on shining shoes.

Where were the manners of the young, he wondered.

31

THAT MORNING, on a large ranch outside Havana, two separate convoys of Mercedes arrived within minutes of each other.

The first contained the president, Raul Castro. In the second was Ramon Suárez, a younger general in his fifties.

The estate was one of the homes of Fidel Castro. Several locations were said to be Fidel's home, so there was always confusion as to his exact whereabouts. This was deliberate, a security measure.

Anyway, today he was here.

"Should we say good morning to Fidel?" asked Suárez. He was related to Fidel Castro by marriage but that was not a license to be familiar with the great man.

"Let's see how he is," said Raul.

A white uniformed nurse led them out to a verandah overlooking an expanse of green lawn to tall trees beyond. The ninety year old former president sat in a chair with a blanket over his knees. A rattan table at his elbow carried a glass of water and a box of tissues. His beard was grey and wispy and his once vigorous frame thin and emaciated.

"Here's Raul to see you," said the nurse cheerfully. Fidel looked up and half raised an arm but did not speak.

"He didn't have a good night," the nurse said in an aside, but loud enough for Fidel to hear.

Raul's round bespectacled face showed sympathy. He patted his older brother's shoulder, muttering a brief word of encouragement, then ushered Suárez away.

In a reception room they sat at a conference table with several assistants, all in uniform, none below the rank of colonel.

"Lots to discuss, let's get started," said Raul.

The agenda included a progress report on the new deep water port at Mariel, a massive project with which Suárez was involved as head of GAESA, the group within the army that controlled most state-owned industry in Cuba. They got through that quickly and then Raul dismissed everyone except Suárez.

"Let's talk about my retirement," he said. He had

previously announced that he would not be a candidate for President in the 2018 elections less than two years away. "I'm thinking about our relations with the Americans."

"Of course."

"I want them to think of us as a country moving towards free speech and democracy, not as a military dictatorship."

"I just want the U.S. embargo to be lifted." Suárez was thinking about his deep water port.

"What about your man Cruz?"

Suárez frowned. "He's not my man. He approached me, not the other way around."

"It would help Cuba's image to have a president who is not a member of the armed forces."

"The First Vice President passes that test," said Suárez.

"Diáz-Canel? I know. But he's associated with the present system. I don't know if having him as President would provide the necessary separation. U.S. politics are such a partisan mess that any excuse will suffice to keep Cuba isolated."

"What are you suggesting? Surely not Cruz as president?"

"Why not?"

Suárez paused a long time, getting his thoughts in order.

"Cruz is an odd man. Very ambitious, and not averse to violence."

He paused, aware that Castro was looking at him with a half smile.

"Sounds like a few people I could name." The President's face split in a grin. "Starting with my brother."

"If we put Cruz in office we would have a hard time controlling him."

Castro was serious again. "I'm just saying don't dismiss the idea. What did he want when he approached you?"

"Money."

Castro shook his head and got up, signifying the meeting's end. "Keep him on a short leash. Don't discourage him but don't give him money, it sends the wrong message."

Suárez was not surprised. After Raul had emerged from his brother's shadow it became clear to those around him that he was, as he had always been, a good organiser, a genial companion, fundamentally ruthless and a man who knew the value of a peso.

32

"HERE'S TO THE TOURIST ECONOMY," muttered Bruno, sucking on a mango.

We were having breakfast on the guest house terrace.

A waitress brought us bread. A delicious smell of baking came from the kitchen.

I buttered a roll, grateful that in Cuba butter meant butter, not spreadable soy-based substitute.

Bruno's phone rang. He listened, replying in monosyllables, then looked at me. I could tell it was not good news.

"That was one of my suppliers in Havana. He lives in the Miramar district, not far from Martin Sanchez Madera's place. Martin's been arrested."

I did not ask who Bruno's informant was. Bruno was part of an extensive grapevine and if he said the

Havana academic had been picked up it was almost certainly true.

"What happened?"

"The police came to his apartment after dark."

I pondered the news. It wasn't a complete surprise, given the man's political activism. But the timing was a shock and surely no coincidence. Had someone been watching him? Could they have seen him talking to Bruno and me on the University campus?

"So now Kon and Sanchez Madera are both prisoners," I said.

"Sounds that way."

"Will they take Martin to the island, too?"

"There's a so-called police training centre outside Cienfuegos. He might be there."

"We should rescue him."

"That may not be possible."

"We have to try. How well guarded is the training facility?"

Bruno looked grave. "Very. Don't kid yourself. Fidel set the place up and he was obsessed with security. It was his number one priority. That's how he survived fifty years of attempted assassinations, including many by agents of the United States."

"Have things relaxed under Raul?" I asked.

"Not really. He may not have his brother's charisma but he's pretty ruthless. He's also better organised. Cuba may be a small country compared to the States but when it comes to security we're major league."

"You're so optimistic."

He shrugged. "One must face facts."

It seemed craven not to try and help Sanchez Madera but, given what Bruno said, I couldn't see a way.

An assault on the island, on the other hand, seemed at least feasible. It was fair to assume the garrison would be modest in size – smaller than at the training facility. And the helicopter assault by Pedro Macias' commandos would be unexpected and would take place out of sight of land. Hopefully it would be all over before more forces could arrive from the mainland.

I explained my reasoning to Bruno, leaving out the part about the helicopter.

"I'm glad you feel that way," he said. "To attack the training centre would be suicidal and I'm not quite ready to die for my country."

Under each table on the terrace of the Magnolia Guest House was a small Japanese microphone. The guest house had been spruced up for tourism several years before. The work was done by a government department which installed the sensors as a matter of course.

The signal went to a recorder in the manager's office. The microphone picked up Oliver's conversation with Bruno clearly although it was not sensitive enough to capture his telephone discussion with Kathy.

The manager didn't listen to the recordings until several hours later, by which time Oliver and Bruno were back on the road. But when he did he called Cruz in Cienfuegos.

"You need to hear this."

Cruz listened, incredulous. "So this pair of clowns is planning to invade the island and liberate Feaver?"

"That's how it sounds."

"Can you describe their vehicle?"

"I am sorry, *Jefe*, we did not see the vehicle, they parked it elsewhere."

"Never mind." They would probably be in the white van that the guayabera man had described, thought Cruz.

"Are they armed?"

"Not as far as I know."

Cruz was irritated. "But you *don't* know, do you."

"No, *Jefe*."

"Very well."

"Did I do right, *Jefe*?"

"Yes, yes. Thank you."

Cruz was not overly disturbed by what he had been told. But he didn't dismiss it either.

The pair would be armed, of course. And although he didn't know anything about this character Sinbad, the man operated in a dangerous business so he shouldn't be taken lightly. On the other hand, the garrison on the island was more than capable of dealing with any attack.

It did not take him long to make up his mind. Rather than give lengthy orders to his lieutenant on Cayo Piedra, he would take command himself. It had been a while since he had been to the island and a visit would encourage the troops. He could also prepare a warm reception for the invaders. He assumed they had access to the same information as Sanchez Madera and, if so, they could not be allowed to remain free.

He must move quickly if he was to get to the island and be ready when they arrived. There was always a launch waiting, moored at the police jetty and he summoned his sergeant.

"I'm going to Cayo Piedra. I have a little business at the Training Centre to take care of first, but then be ready to leave as soon as I say."

33

"I'm glad to be getting out of this joint," I said as we left the guest house.

"Getting nervous?" asked Bruno.

"I'm not sure why. There's something about the place." I got behind the wheel.

"I don't think you need worry," he said. "Although, in Cuba you can never be sure."

"See if you can raise Sinbad," I suggested.

A rapid stream of Spanish told me contact was made. Bruno put a hand over the phone and turned to me.

"He's still at sea, but on schedule."

"How will we find him?"

More Spanish.

Then, "There is a bay ten miles west of the city. I know it. He'll meet us there."

"What time? Neither of us wants to be loafing around waiting for the other."

"Of course," said Bruno. "Name a time after nightfall and he'll meet it."

"From here, our timing must be precise," I said. "How long will it take to get to the island?"

"It depends on wind and tide."

"Give me an estimate?"

He shrugged. "Sixty to ninety minutes."

I looked at my watch, it was two pm. If we met Sinbad without incident and left the mainland promptly we could reach the island by eight.

Everything depended on the helicopter reaching the island at exactly that time. The problem was that we couldn't communicate with it once it was in the air so we had to establish a schedule and stick to it rigorously.

It would take the helicopter a little over two hours to cover the 350 miles from the Everglades to Cayo Piedra. I would tell them to be there at eight and urge them in the strongest terms to be on time.

"Tell Sinbad 6:30 and not to be late," I told Bruno.

Sinbad must have said something amusing because Bruno laughed nervously before ringing off. "This is going to require pretty much perfect timing," he said.

"You're right, but it's the only plan we have. We have to make it happen."

Next, I called Kathy on Tortola.

"Hello?" Her reassuring American accent.

"It's me." I explained the situation. "Where is Carlton?"

"He's down at the boatyard working on *Guinevere*. Are you going to rescue Sanchez Madera as well as Kon?" It was her first question.

"I don't know if we can."

"You have to try, at least."

I explained as patiently as I could that it was not possible. She did not say much but her silence was eloquent. I changed the subject.

"I need you to talk to Carlton urgently. Tell him that tonight's a go."

"For sure?"

"Yes. We're reasonably confident that we shall link up with Sinbad and reach the island on time."

"Reasonably?"

"That's what I said. Tell Carlton to make sure Pedro's people are ready in every respect. The chopper must arrive on the stroke of eight, come hell or high water."

"Hold on, I'll call him now. I'll put the two phones side by side, then you can talk to Carlton direct."

But that was too ambitious. All I could hear was static so we reverted to the relay system. I gave her messages which she passed on to Carlton, repeating his answers back to me.

"He suggests the helicopter should leave half an hour earlier than you said, to allow for the unforeseen."

"Okay. If they're early they can circle around when they get close to the island. Make it clear that if it's even a minute late, Bruno and I will probably be dead ducks."

I heard her repeat that to Carlton.

"He says *Buena Suerte*, Good luck."

"Tell him to wish Pedro's group the same," I said.

"You take care."

We drove on south.

34

"WE MADE GOOD TIME," said Bruno a few hours later. "I'll drive through the city."

We were approaching Cienfuegos, a coastal city of 150,000 souls and the capital of Cienfuegos province.

The streets were broad and attractive and the neo-classical buildings in good condition by Cuban standards. In the main square I admired a white marble statue of José Marti, writer and liberator of Cuba in the War of Independence.

We reached the ocean. Bruno pointed to a large mansion facing out to sea. "That was once a rich merchant's villa; now it's the regional police headquarters. Cruz probably has an office there."

"Better not stop," I said. "This would be a bad time to be booked for loitering."

Bruno drove west along the coast. We reached a rural area about ten miles from the town and took a turning that led through woods for several miles and then to the beach. I noted with approval that it was remote and well away from curious eyes.

Bruno steered the van off the road. Using scattered patches of dry ground, he drove into a clearing where he braked and turned to me.

"We'll leave the van here. The beach is only five minutes walk."

"Good work," I said. "Call Sinbad again."

He took out his phone. "Hola Sinbad."

Evidently things were on course because he turned to me, excited.

"He's two miles offshore. He's been marking time there for half an hour. He doesn't want to hang around any longer in case the coastguard notice him, so he's coming in."

"Let's scramble then." I grabbed the suitcase with my map, phone and computer. Not much to fight a war with.

When we reached the beach, Bruno rolled up his trouser legs. "You'll have to get your feet wet. The boat draws about two feet of water. The beach shelves for a while and then drops off sharply, thirty yards out. That's where he'll be."

Sinbad appeared, right on time. We waded out as the boat chugged towards us. It turned broadside on and stopped. We threw our bags to Sinbad and he caught them and handed us on board.

With Sinbad's deckhand José at the wheel the boat described a wide arc and headed south.

"Ask Sinbad if he knows the way," I told Bruno. The grizzled sailor obviously understood because he grinned and spread his arms as if to say, 'no idea.'

"He grew up helping his dad, who was a fisher-man," said Bruno. "He's at home in these seas."

I nodded to Sinbad and pointed at my wrist-watch. "Eight o'clock. We must arrive at eight o'clock exactly."

He nodded. "No problem."

We sat at the cabin table and I spread out the paper with my sketch of the island.

"Bruno and I will steal up on the office building, here," I tapped with my pencil, "and get hold of their keys. There should only be a couple of guards there and they won't be expecting us so we'll have the advantage of surprise."

Sinbad's eyes met mine. "Piece of cake," he said in English. I was beginning to get his sense of humour.

"We don't know which cell Kon is in. He may not be in a cell at all, but in *la caja* – the box. We should look there first," I said.

"How will we know which is the correct key?"

asked Bruno. "We could waste valuable minutes fiddling with different keys."

"I have a plan for that," I said. "But if he's not in the box our task becomes harder. In that case we'll have to go to the cell block and try to figure out which door and which key to use."

Sinbad nodded. "I wait for you in the boat."

"If we're not back in thirty minutes you have my permission to leave without us. Go home and forget the whole thing."

He shook his head. "I wait."

35

"THIS IS SO PEACEFUL," said Kathy. She and Mimi were sitting by the pool on Tortola, nursing Margaritas.

Mimi nodded. "Sure is."

"Do you think it's like this where Oliver is?" asked Kathy.

"Probably."

"How far is Cuba?"

"About five hundred miles. It's a bit cooler than here, but not much."

It was late afternoon but the sun was still well above the horizon. The temperature was Tortola's usual eighty degrees. Far below, silver highlights danced on waves stirred by a warm breeze. The sea had not yet taken on the glassy sheen that would come with dusk and the new moon.

They could hear Carlton talking in his den.

"He's speaking to a broker in Los Angeles. They're plotting some kind of arbitrage deal between Wall Street and Tokyo and it's getting tricky."

"Never lets up, does he?"

"Nope," said Mimi. "Gotta put bread on the table."

"Oliver says he can manage without any help."

"They always say that."

"It's difficult not knowing what's going on."

"Who's he dealing with down there?" Mimi asked.

"Someone called Bruno. He's Kon's contact in Havana – a wheeler dealer. Kon said he's great if you want a black market TV, but hardly a reliable ally."

"What's their plan?"

"It's a high risk operation," said Kathy. "Kon is on a prison island somewhere between Cuba and the Caymans, locked up in dreadful conditions. Oliver and Bruno are going to access the island in a twin-pronged surprise attack – by sea and air. They are the seaborne force, in a boat belonging to a guy called Sinbad."

"Who's the air force?"

"A group of freedom fighters assembled by Pedro Macias. They will leave the Everglades by helicopter and take control of the prison yard while Oliver and Bruno sneak in and rescue Kon."

"Sounds high-risk," said Mimi.

"Sounds plumb crazy."

"The timing must be synchronised to the second or there could be big problems."

"I know that," said Kathy. She got up and paced across the patio. "I ought to be there. Not on the front line perhaps, but in reserve. Someone will need to bring them back if they're successful. I could do that."

"When, not if."

"Huh?"

"*When* they're successful."

"Of course." A tear rolled down her cheek and she brushed it away. "I get so annoyed with that stupid Britisher."

Mimi sat up. "Whoa, where did that come from?"

"He won't listen to advice. He knows all about numbers I suppose, but it's not enough just to be a clever accountant."

"Carlton thinks he's smart, and my husband has high standards."

"That's fine, but you also need judgment if you're going to put yourself in serious danger."

Mimi nodded. "That stubborn attitude goes with a certain kind of British education. Fear God Honour the Queen, boarding school and so on.

"He's so rigid."

"If it's any consolation, Brits of that sort are

usually capable of extreme deviousness, the more effective because it's unexpected," said Mimi.

"You mean like when he talked that homicidal South African into jumping off a thirtieth floor balcony at the Shard?" (see *Casino Qaddafi*)

"Exactly."

Kathy sniffed. "I just hope he knows what he's doing."

Mimi wrapped her arms round Kathy and gave her a hug. Kathy returned it and Mimi kissed her.

"I'm sure he does."

Kathy did not reply. She went indoors and used her tablet computer to research the procedure for U.S. citizens visiting Cuba.

The rules had been relaxed following a recent executive order by President Obama. Even so, she would be required to conform to a programme of cultural exchanges with Cubans. A nice idea, but constricting because she would be expected to follow a planned schedule. She looked up a couple of travel agents that offered such tours and telephoned them.

Her question was simple. "How can I travel to Cuba *now*?"

The first agency, a big outfit, were polite but firm. "The visa will take a week. You'll need to travel with us, stay in the hotels we select and attend events arranged by the Cuban Tourist Ministry."

"I'll get back to you," she said.

The other agency was based in Brighton Beach, New York. Yes, there was paperwork but they had an 'in' at the Consulate and if she applied now they could process her quickly. They made so many promises it made her nervous, but she took the risk and spent half an hour downloading forms.

"Where do I sign?" she asked.

"Leave them blank," said Boris the agent whose accent might have been Russian. "Just email us a scanned copy of the signature page of your passport."

A nod and a wink, she thought. Her signature would magically appear on the required line, and would match her passport. She felt apprehensive about the risk of identity theft but she decided to chance it.

Boris called her back an hour later. All was in order. The group would meet at a hotel in Tampa tomorrow but she must pay four thousand dollars now. She gave her Mastercard details and waited nervously.

He came back in seconds. "You're all set. Have a wonderful time!"

We'll see about that, she thought. She ran next door to Mimi. "I'm going."

"Going where?"

She consulted her notes. "José Marti Airport,

Havana. Can you give me a ride to the airport, first thing tomorrow?"

"Oh my god."

36

THEY GOT to Tortola's small airport early next morning.

Instead of waving her goodbye, Mimi parked the Jeep in the car park, took a travel bag from the trunk and walked to the terminal with her.

"What's this?" asked Kathy.

"I'm coming too. Did you think you were going to hog all the fun?"

"But you can't do that," Kathy stammered.

"Who says?"

"I mean, I'd love you to but it's not that easy. You need a visa and loads of paperwork."

"Not true, girlfriend. You forget I'm a British citizen."

"So?"

"So I shall fly to Toronto or Cozumel, one or the other, and buy a ticket to Havana. The airline will issue a visa with the ticket automatically. Very simple, and all perfectly legal."

37

CALEB HADN'T REALLY EXPECTED to hear back, after his singing audition. So he got a jolt of optimism when a few days later there was a message on his elderly mobile phone. It was his interviewer Pepe.

'Be at Café Hola tonight at seven,' were the terse words.

The café was in a marginal part of town but beggars can't be choosers, he told himself. He hadn't heard of the place before, so when he got there he was not surprised to learn that it had only been open a week. A gaudy neon sign in the style of "Tropicana" fifty years ago flickered on and off, shedding febrile red, blue and yellow light on the shabby buildings to either side.

The building was a converted warehouse. It looked as if a substantial sum had been spent doing it up and Caleb wondered where the money had come from. Tables and chairs and a bar had been installed plus a stage at one end of the room. It looked forlorn in daylight but he knew that when darkness fell and spotlights bathed the stage the necessary atmosphere could soon be created. The sound equipment was of reasonable quality. There was not enough space for a large band so he guessed the cheaper alternative of a recorded backing plus guitars, trumpet and maracas would be used.

He was the first to arrive but other members of the group began to appear until there were six of them, five men and a woman.

He recognised several faces. Like him they had been on the fringe of the entertainment community and he suspected that, also like him, they were glad to be working at all. Eduardo was short, with black curly hair, and, when not on stage, a morose manner; he had a decent voice but Caleb had never liked him much. David had a quirky sense of humour but a thin voice. Neither had managed to break into the front rank of entertainers as the tourist economy grew. They were a bit younger than Caleb and dressed like him. He also recognised several members of the band which consisted of keyboard, two guitarists and percussion and it was not hard to spot the theme which was modelled closely on the Buena Vista Social Club.

The woman Amanda was younger, in her forties, blonde and pale skinned. She was motherly and cheerful. Her dress was off the shoulder with a lot of glitter and while not fat she was well built with a generous bosom that the dress showed to advantage. Caleb had shared a stage with her before. He strolled over.

"This is an odd setup." He indicated the empty hall.

"Hi, Caleb. Yes, you're right, but so what? It's better than nothing."

"Who's really behind it?"

"Not that dreadful Pepe, I'm sure." She grimaced and he laughed.

"He said an American was putting the money up."

"Is that legal?" she asked.

"Probably not, but there are ways of fixing that sort of thing."

"Well it's work and I have two kids to feed."

Word was her husband was no longer around but that it was just as well. He was violent and had beaten her.

"For sure."

The audience began to trickle in and the house was half full when the lights went down at nine. Soft drinks and watery *Mojitos* were available from the makeshift bar, and some basic snacks which to Caleb looked second rate. Pepe was there. Caleb watched him bustling round, officious and demanding, ordering stage hands to rearrange the banners festooning the simple stage and making sure the kitchen was organised to provide a flow of drinks and food. The Pepes of this world might lack charm but he had to admit the fellow had his uses.

The crowd were mostly foreigners, in holiday mood and not disposed to be too critical. There were Canadians, Germans and other Europeans plus a sprinkling from the U.S. Eavesdropping, Caleb gathered they had been turned on to the event by reception at various second rank hotels – the bigger places would probably not favour an upstart venture like this over established clubs like the Parisien or the Tropicana.

After a slow start, enthusiasm built up – the audience was in a mood to be generous although some older members did not seem to enjoy the loud amplification or the singers' uncompromisingly direct delivery and a few couples got up and left early.

The performance was nonstop. After half an hour the singers were really into things despite not having sung as a group before and belted out a series of popular favourites. Cheap rum flowed in the warm evening and the air grew thick with cigar smoke. The beat got more assured while the singers, relaxed and smiling, achieved a lilting wistfulness that evoked the old pre-Castro days.

Afterwards, even officious Pepe seemed pleased as he paid the performers, counting out grubby notes in the empty hall.

Caleb stood at the bus stop with Amanda, waiting for a ride home.

"I enjoyed that," he said. "I didn't know what to expect, but it was fun."

"The crowd had a good time," she said.

He thought of the money in his pocket. "I guess we're finally part of the tourist economy."

She nodded drily. "Every Cuban's dream."

"Long may it last."

38

"You look terrific, Kathy" said Brittany the tour guide. She was slightly surprised to see a well dressed beauty travelling alone. Her parties consisted mostly of couples or older singles, not twenty-five year old blondes.

Kathy smiled. "Why thank you."

"You're just in time. Come down to the coffee shop for my introductory spiel."

Kathy and Mimi had flown to San Juan on a Cape Air six-passenger Cessna. Each of them had to state their weight before boarding so as to balance the small airplane. After a short twenty minute flight to San Juan they had parted company. Mimi caught an onward flight to Toronto while Kathy flew to Tampa where she checked into the Crowne Plaza hotel.

At the meeting, Brittany ran through some dos and don'ts, then asked, "Any questions?"

A woman raised her hand.

"I've heard that Cuba is a police state. How should we handle the police?"

Brittany laughed. "Same way you would in the U.S. The mood in Cuba is pretty normal. In fact, life in Havana is safer than right here. You can walk down the street at night without getting mugged. It's an orderly place and the police are friendly."

If she only knew, thought Kathy back in her room. She looked through her papers and saw they would be staying at a hotel on Cayo Santa Maria, a twenty mile long causeway off the north coast a hundred miles east of Havana.

She telephoned Mimi.

"Where are you?" she asked.

"At a Holiday Inn in Toronto."

"Any good?"

"It's clean and close to the airport."

Kathy sensed her non-enthusiasm. "When are you leaving?"

"Crack of dawn tomorrow."

"How did it go with the visa?"

"No problem."

"Where will you be staying in Havana?"

"At the Hotel Nacional."

"Is that the grand old joint, the one where the mob guys used to stay?"

"And Sinatra, yeah that's the place."

"Call me when you get there."

"Where will you be?"

"The Residencia Magnifica on Cayo Santa Maria, wherever that is."

"Sounds like an island. What's the phone number there?"

Kathy reached for the documents Brittany had handed out. She looked for a number but could not see one.

"It's not here. I'll have to call you later."

"Okay. Sleep well."

"You too. This is shaping up to be exciting."

"I hope not," said Mimi.

Kathy arrived in Cuba around noon the next day. Havana's Jose Martí airport was small by U.S. standards and not very modern. She had to walk down steps to get off the airplane – none of those tubular walkways that get passengers straight into the lobby. The warm air was humid as she strolled across the tarmac and it started to rain as she ducked into the terminal building.

"How much money should I change?" she asked Brittany.

"Not a lot. You can get more at the hotel. The rate's the same everywhere."

She changed a hundred dollars and was pleased to see that the rate was fixed and no commission was charged, a welcome difference from the U.S. where exchange outfits gouged the customer outrageously.

The party boarded a coach.

"We have several hour's drive to get to Cayo Santa Maria," said Brittany.

The air conditioned vehicle swished through the countryside past fields of tobacco and sugarcane. The scenery was green and attractive. But she was shocked by the condition of the houses along the road which were mostly drab unpainted shacks, a sign of serious poverty. But the people she glimpsed seemed relaxed enough.

"Not many fat people," she said to Brittany.

"That's not surprising. In Cuba, food is rationed. Everyone has a ration book and gets a monthly allowance of groceries at reduced price. After that they have to pay full price for anything they buy."

"How do they manage?"

"With difficulty. Nobody who works for the state has any spare money. In the countryside there's a lot of unofficial to and fro, people grow their own vegetables and barter livestock between one farm and another, stuff like that."

"Aren't people resentful?"

"Yes and no. Things have been that way for so long that most folk accept it because it's all they know."

"And the weather's good," she said.

"And Fidel is a hero who stood up to the wicked Americans."

They drove for some miles along a coast road, past more of the simple hovels Kathy was coming to regard as the norm. Then they stopped at a security barrier manned by armed police in blue and grey. A swarthy guard spoke briefly to the driver before waving them through and the coach swung onto a narrow causeway that seemed to head straight out to sea.

"Get ready for a change of pace," said Brittany.

"Meaning?"

"You'll see."

Fifteen miles along the sandy causeway they came to a handsome formal entrance announcing the "Residencia Magnifica." The coach slowed and turned in. It drove half a mile along a smooth gravel driveway with clipped hedges on either side and ornamental lamp posts at intervals. Everything was immaculately kept, in sharp contrast with the poverty on the mainland.

"Welcome to the new Cuba – tourist version," said Brittany.

An ornamental fountain played in the middle of a vast lobby. The marble floor was dotted with expensive sofas and coffee tables. It was like stepping into a palace. Pretty waitresses marched to and fro with drinks on trays.

Kathy registered at the desk. She was then directed outside where an electric golf cart was waiting with her bags already loaded. She climbed aboard and the cart swished along winding paths through the shrubbery to a two storey cottage-style villa, one of many in the grounds. Her magnetic key card opened the door to a large ground floor suite with a spotless king sized bed.

She took in the big flat panel television with a channel guide that listed CNN and BBC World News as well as a number of Spanish stations which she assumed were Mexican or South American. She turned the set on and tuned it to CNN. There were Wolf Blitzer and Christiane Amanpour holding forth. Cuba might be a police state but it didn't seem too concerned about censorship.

In the gleaming bathroom she ran the hot tap and it gushed scalding water. There was a coffee maker, an iron, a hairdryer and a combination safe in the wardrobe.

It feels like Las Vegas, she thought. She half expected slot machines and blackjack tables in the lobby. She wondered if the developers had that in mind when they designed the place. She guessed it was government-owned but managed by an overseas company and her guess was confirmed when she studied the labels on the shampoo bottle and the soap wrapper and saw the logo of a leading Spanish hotel chain.

It was nice to be surrounded by modern comforts, but she had work to do. First, communications. She read the telephone instructions and pressed 9 for an outside line, then dialled the Hotel Nacional. She asked to be put through to Mimi.

"Hola!" It was Mimi.

"I like the accent. This is your spy from Cayo Santa Maria."

"Well I'm in Havana."

What's the Nacional like?"

"Old fashioned. The public areas are lovely. Art deco exterior. Inside, polished wood and gleaming brass. Bloody great picture of Fidel in the lobby and a bookstore full of badly printed anti-U.S. pamphlets. Gorgeous terrace overlooking the Malecon. The bedrooms are a bit poky, though. What do we do now?"

"That depends," said Kathy. "I'm going to phone Oliver. Wait to hear from me, I'll call you back."

She dialled Oliver's mobile number, using the

US area code first, since his phone probably thought it was still in the United States.

"Hello?" His voice was guarded, but surprisingly clear.

"The cavalry is here," she said.

He drew a sharp breath. "I told you not to come."

"No you didn't. You said you didn't need help."

"Well I don't."

"Maybe not yet," she said. "Where are you?"

"We're on our way to Cayo Piedra."

"We?"

"Bruno and me."

"To release Kon?"

"That's the plan."

"Defying shedloads of armed guards?"

"Something like that. We'll break the good news to them that the counter revolution is here and they'll all crowd round and kiss us."

"From your lips to God's ears."

"Martin Sanchez Madera's kidnapping is a problem, though."

"Was he an important informant?"

"Yes. I was counting on him to help us with the political stuff. I called his house again to talk to his wife but she doesn't know much. She was beside herself with anxiety."

"I can get someone to go and see her."

"I thought you were on Cayo Santa Maria. That's a long way from Havana."

"I'll call our man in Havana. Our woman, actually."

"Tell me you're joking."

"I told you the cavalry was here."

39

MIMI TISCH RANG the doorbell of the small Miramar apartment.

"Who is it?"

"A friend of Martin."

A tear-stained Sylvia Sanchez Madera opened the door a crack. Mimi stood outside. Sylvia stared at her but apparently decided she was not a threat because she opened the door wider and let her in.

She poured Mimi a glass of water and they sat at the kitchen table.

Sylvia was in her late twenties, dark haired and attractive. She spoke excellent English but was very subdued at first. Mimi explained her connection with Oliver Steele and so with Martin Sanchez Madera. She did not know how to continue the conversation but she didn't need to, because after a brief hesitation Sylvia's feelings came pouring out.

"I knew about Martin's political activity of course," she said between sniffs. "I'm not stupid. I knew that when the Castros went he would become even more active politically but I didn't realise it would happen so soon. I thought he was still just laying groundwork, collecting information."

"Did you know about his trip to Florida?"

She nodded. "Yes. That terrified me."

"Why? I've heard that it's no big deal if you're caught trying to leave Cuba. You just pay a fine."

"That's true for most people. But my husband is – how can I put it – a high profile figure. He is prominent at the University. For people like him the stakes are higher. Being arrested will mean prison or worse."

"I thought things were freer since Fidel stepped down?"

She shook her head. "Raul is no better than his brother. In the early days of the revolution he was thoroughly ruthless and old habits die hard. Now, just as before, the State can be merciless if it thinks someone well known is getting out of line. "

"Do you think the State has finally lost patience with Martin?"

"Well someone has, either the State or somebody else."

"What do you mean?"

"The State isn't the only threat. There are other forces."

"Such as?"

"People jockeying for position in the new order. Doing what Martin was trying to do, but for selfish reasons. Martin just wants to bring democracy to Cuba, but these other people . . !" She shuddered in disgust.

"And now the police have your husband?"

She nodded. "Yes, although I think it may be a particular individual within the police."

"Meaning?"

She led Mimi to a desk and unlocked a drawer. "Martin keeps files on what he calls 'the opposition' – people he thinks will resist democratic government after the Castros." She smiled sadly. "He's a great record keeper."

She pulled out a folder, one of several.

"The worst example is Hector Cruz. I think he's the man who took my husband. He is commander of the police district that includes the provinces of Villa Clara and Cienfuegos, so he's in charge of much of central Cuba."

"Why do you suspect him?"

"Martin was friends with Pavel, a young Russian who lives down the street from here. A few weeks ago, he told Martin that a manager in the embassy was working a scam with a Cuban police officer."

"What sort of scam?"

She shook her head. "Something to do with spare parts for police vehicles. They were faking paperwork and overbilling the government."

"I'm surprised an auditor would be so indiscreet."

"Perhaps, but the younger generation of Russians is different. He may have thought that by talking to Martin he was helping both Russia and Cuba. Anyway, soon afterwards, he was killed in a late night so-called traffic accident."

"Which you think was no accident?"

Sylvia nodded.

"How did Cruz operate?" asked Mimi.

"He was using money from the scam to bribe his lieutenants."

Mimi nodded. "That's a common kleptocrat technique."

"And people are poor here, so a little money goes a long way."

Mimi leafed through the folder. Her Spanish was good enough for her to get the gist of the notes in Sanchez Madera's neat handwriting. He had drawn little maps and diagrams and an organisational chart of the Villa Clara police force with red arrows showing the flow of money.

"How did he get so much detail?"

"He had other informants besides Pavel."

"Really?"

"When he started to focus on Cruz, he set about cultivating links with members of the police. He found one who Cruz had passed over, who bore him a grudge."

She paused. "Also, Cruz has a girlfriend who works in a cigar factory, Teresita. Martin got valuable information from her."

Mimi raised her eyebrows and Sylvia smiled. "I know how that sounds but Martin's very proper. He would never cheat on me."

"Good to know," said Mimi.

40

MIMI FINISHED her drink and got up to leave. On an impulse she took Sylvia's hand.

"You're very brave, but I think you should get away from here," she said.

"Why?"

"Because if I know anything it won't be long before Cruz comes looking for his file."

Sylvia looked confused. "Where would I go?"

Mimi shrugged. "Somewhere not obvious. Don't go straight to your mother."

"I have cousins I seldom see who live on a farm near Santiago. That's in the far eastern part of the island, a long way from here."

"That sounds good."

"I'll phone them now."

"I wouldn't do that," said Mimi quickly. "It might

leave a trail. Just go and catch the bus. It sounds as if they will be glad to see you, so it'll be a pleasant surprise for them."

Sylvia looked at a loss. "What about this file on Cruz? Should I give it to the authorities?"

"Which authorities? You don't know whose side they are on, or what the heck is going on in government circles nowadays. You might empower someone just as bad as Cruz."

"What, then?"

An idea had been dawning on Mimi. She didn't like it but it was starting to seem like the only solution.

"Give it to me," she said.

Sylvia frowned. "How do I know I can trust you?"

"You don't. But you need to trust someone and I'm the nearest non-police person just at the moment."

Sylvia bundled some belongings for herself and her husband into a suitcase. Half an hour later she was on her way to the bus station to catch a long distance coach to Santiago.

Meanwhile, Mimi was back in her room at the Nacional, staring at the combination safe in the bottom of the clothes closet, in which she had just locked the Hector Cruz file. What the heck had she gotten herself into?

41

"How did it go?" Kathy asked Mimi, who was out of breath.

She had just got back to her room and had broken into a run when she heard the phone ringing.

"Okay, I guess," she said. "But Martin Sanchez Madera is in trouble, that's for sure."

"What's his wife like?"

"Very nice, but desperately worried."

"What did you learn that we can use?"

"Hector Cruz has a compound in Cienfuegos where he's accumulating an arsenal."

"For when the time comes?"

"Right. He's a thorough-going fascist. He only believes in two things – brute force and money."

"How has he got so powerful without the authorities knowing?"

"To most ordinary people, he *is* the authorities. Apart from a few key cronies, his people think they are discharging normal government business, so there's no cause for suspicion."

"When does he plan to make his move?"

"As soon as the new government takes office after the 2018 election."

"Will he have popular support?"

"He won't need it. As far as the average Cuban is concerned there will be a palace revolution, something only affecting a few people at the top, none of whom have a strong popular following. Remember, the upcoming election is not real, not the kind of election we're used to in the States. It's just a way to rubber stamp a Castro-approved successor."

"Someone like the First Vice President?"

"He's a probable."

"But his reign would be short?"

"If Cruz has anything to do with it, yes. According to his plan, hours before the new president is due to address the nation, police units will move into the presidential office. There may be shooting but it will be short and sweet thanks to the element of surprise. The president-elect will be arrested, led away and probably never seen again.

Cruz will come forward in his place and announce that the president has stepped down due to ill health, and has nominated trusted police commander Hector Cruz as his successor."

"Will people believe that?"

"It won't matter what they believe. It'll be a fait accompli, announced in a calm, low key way. Life will go on."

"Then what?"

"Cruz has it all worked out. He'll double the minimum wage for state employees – that's seven out of ten Cubans. He also plans to increase the food ration by fifty percent so that people will regard him gratefully."

"Where will he get the money to do all this?"

"He'll print it."

"What about food?" Kathy was thinking about the ration books. "Won't there be shortages?"

"Probably, but they won't bite – excuse the pun – until later. By then Cruz will have consolidated his position. And if some people starve, too bad! He'll be firmly in charge."

"So there will be dictatorship all over again?"

"That's about it. An old style dictatorship replacing a communist dictatorship. Not much difference really."

"We should tell Oliver about the Cienfuegos headquarters," said Kathy.

"Where is he?"

"Somewhere on the way to the prison island, Cayo Piedra."

42

HELL AND DAMNATION, thought Sylvia Sanchez Madera. She marched along the street looking neither to right nor left.

Her suitcase was heavy and a couple of times she tripped on one of the many holes in the Havana sidewalk and almost fell but eventually she reached the bus station, hot and out of breath.

The line was short, half a dozen people preparing, like herself, for a long journey. She surrendered her suitcase, telling the porter her destination and he stowed it away in the rear of the baggage hold at the bottom of the bus. She found a seat and peered out of the dusty window as the elderly vehicle pulled away and rumbled through the streets of suburban Havana.

She finally began to relax as they left the city

behind and the scenery changed to fields and villages. She should have brought something to eat, she thought – it was a twelve hour journey with only a handful of stops and she could have saved money by packing something.

After an hour and a half, the bus pulled off the main road and into Jagüey Grande, a modest sized town surrounded by citrus groves, for a scheduled stop. Sylvia awoke from a doze as they jolted to a halt.

The door opened and a man boarded. He wore the grey shirt and blue trousers of the PNR. He surveyed the half-empty bus, eyes moving from person to person.

She realised uneasily that she was one of only two unaccompanied women on board. The other woman was older, lined, a grandmother? Her expression was one of disinterest mixed with relief when she was passed over. Nobody likes to be the object of attention of the police.

The trooper clearly knew what he was looking for because his gaze reached Sylvia and stayed there. "Sylvia Sanchez Madera?" His face was impassive.

How to react? Be natural. She smiled and nodded. "That's me."

"Come with me, please."

"May I ask why?"

"Please step off."

Clutching her purse she rose and walked down the aisle.

It was late afternoon and starting to grow dark outside. No real bus station, not even a sign, just a drab general store. Apparently everyone in Jagüey Grande knew where the bus stopped.

A car was parked by the side of the road with another policeman behind the wheel.

"What's this about?" She kept her voice steady.

"Nothing major, just a few questions. Do you have a bag?"

Behave naturally! There was nothing controversial in the suitcase anyway and it would seem odd not to claim it. Besides, if she let her belongings go on to Santiago she would certainly never see them again, regardless of her fate.

"It's in the hold."

There was pushing and pulling while the bag was disinterred. Finally, like its owner, it was in the police car being driven away.

The car was followed by the curious gaze of the passengers and crew of the bus and a sprinkling of bystanders. Little curiosity was shown. Such events were unusual but not unknown. If anyone had concerns about the incident, they knew better than to voice them.

43

"NOW THEN," said Cruz, "Who have we here?"

Sylvia stood in front of him. He sat at his desk, looking her up and down.

Her hands were not tied but a guard stood on either side. She had a crazy impulse to seize the gun from one of them and shoot everyone in sight but she had no idea how to use such a weapon. She felt paralyzed.

"You know who I am. Where's my husband?"

Cruz sighed. "I will ask the questions."

"I have nothing to say."

He stood up and strolled over to the window, turning his back on her. He gazed out to sea.

"Your husband is clever. He seems to have collected a lot of information about certain individuals, including me. He has a way with people, apparently. He gets them to confide in him. I admire him for that."

"Then release him."

He shook his head. "It's a shame he has such misguided political ideas."

"Misguided? Is that what you think?"

"He might describe them as democratic. But democracy is a system whose time has not yet come in Cuba." He seemed to be musing aloud. "No, not on this island."

He was goading her but she couldn't help taking the bait. "It's better than your brand of fascism."

He shrugged. "How do you know what I believe? How do you know anything about me?"

He approached and pushed his pale face close to hers, nearly touching. She could see each black hair of the short beard and smell his cologne. She recoiled slightly and he backed off and smiled.

"We searched your apartment. There are files, I know the way he works. But we found nothing about me."

He must have spotted a hint of satisfaction in her eye because he frowned.

"Information about me must not fall into the wrong hands. Meaning the present government."

She bit her tongue. But she couldn't resist spreading her hands in a small gesture as if to say, 'Yes, that would be the end of you.'

Their eyes met in a moment of understanding.

She expected to be tortured. She tried to think of herself as already dead. No matter the pain, she would endure it and if necessary die.

Cruz saw the defiance in her eyes.

"You have courage," he said. "I respect that." To her surprise he put an arm on her shoulder, pressing down so that she was forced to sit on the chair before his desk. He motioned to a guard.

"Bring refreshments. Coffee for both of us, and water."

He sat down in his own chair and took a cigar from a box on the desk, making an elaborate performance of lighting it with a match from a marble holder on the leather desktop. Coffee and iced water arrived.

He smiled. "Drink some water at least. It's not drugged and you must be thirsty."

After a moment's hesitation she sipped from the glass.

Cruz smiled. "We have your husband. He is at a police facility not far from here. And to answer your next question, apart from a few bruises caused by resisting some reasonable restraints, he is unharmed."

"He will tell you nothing," she said, "Neither will I."

He nodded. "Well spoken."

He turned his laptop computer around so that she could see the screen.

"I want you to watch something."

With dismay she peered at the image on the screen. It was her husband, tied to a chair, his face haggard.

Cruz picked up the phone and spoke.

"Give him a tweak. Not strong."

A shadowy figure with its back to the camera moved forward holding calipers at the end of an electrical cord. The figure carefully attached the clip to one of Sanchez Madera's ears. Sanchez Madera flinched but said nothing. The shadow moved out of camera range.

A moment later Sanchez Madera's body jerked violently upwards, straining at the restraints. There was no audio but his face contorted in an obvious scream.

Sylvia let out a cry.

"Now," said Cruz, "I said I respected you, and I do. No doubt your husband will be equally brave. The question is, how long can you watch him being tortured – you see I call a spade a spade, no nonsense about enhanced interrogation – before you give me what I need."

. . .

At that moment, Mimi was in her hotel room in Havana. She had just finished reading Sanchez Madera's file on Cruz. She made some notes on the message pad provided by the hotel and called Oliver.

"What's the scoop?" he asked.

"It's incriminating stuff. Cruz is a piece of work. It describes how he ripped off his own government for years working with this Russian, Igor. That alone would be enough to ruin his career and send him to prison. No wonder he's desperate to get his hands on the file."

"What else does it tell us?"

"There's a big police facility at Cienfuegos. That's where they will probably be, if they are not already on the island."

"Give me coordinates," snapped Oliver. He motioned to Bruno. "Write this down."

44

"WE HEARD FROM CUBA. The operation's a go."

Pedro Macias couldn't conceal his enthusiasm. He was at home in Hialeah, speaking to Luis in the Everglades.

"Yay."

Pedro could almost hear Luis pump his fist. Every ounce of the young patriot's excitement was channelled into his cheer.

"It means taking off very soon. Are you in good shape over there?"

"Sure." Luis made an effort to speak calmly. "We were hoping to hear from you today and we've made our preparations. Weapons are cleaned, locked and loaded. Backpacks checked. We've rehearsed the drills over and over again."

"Excellent," said Pedro.

"I even . . ." Luis's voice tailed off.

"What?"

"I got each of the guys to make a will. Went to the store and bought forms and handed them round. They are just kids, none of them had ever made a will before. Most of them left anything they had to their mom and dad. They gave me a hard time for being nervous. I guess it was silly of me."

"It's not silly," said Pedro. There was a silence.

Pedro asked, "What about the 'copter? Is it reliable? It's not exactly brand new."

"I don't think you need worry about that," said Luis. "I hear what you're saying, but our pilot Bert is a good hand. No spring chicken but he saw service in Afghanistan. Knows the machine and seems to be a savvy mechanic as well as a pilot."

"Good." Pedro paused. "I'll be over to see you shortly."

"You want to come along for the ride?"

Pedro laughed. "No, that's young men's work. But I'll be there to bless you and speed you on your way."

When Pedro got to the Everglades, Luis greeted him with a robust handshake but Pedro thought he detected an undercurrent.

"Is everything okay?" The soldiers all looked organised and ready, lounging on plastic garden furniture that had been imported for the purpose. Some were smoking or sipping sodas. They wore clean fatigues with the Black Eagle patch and had their backpacks and weapons by their sides. For an amateur army in the middle of nowhere it was impressive, Pedro thought.

Over by the helicopter the pilot Bert was crouching on the ground under the great machine's belly holding a spanner and peering up at the fuselage through a hole left by the plate he had removed.

Pedro looked at his watch. It was 5:30, half an hour before takeoff. He strolled over to the pilot, trying to seem calm.

"How's it going?"

Bert went on poking with the screwdriver as if he wanted to adjust something, but didn't know what.

"Tell you shortly."

Pedro wasn't sure if Bert appreciated the seriousness of the time issue so, a few moments later, he said, "The guys should take off in half an hour. Timing is critical."

Bert did not react immediately. When he did, he rolled over, manoeuvred his beer belly away from the machine and looked up at Pedro. He had a round head and a white walrus moustache stained around the mouth with nicotine. He looked about sixty, with piggy eyes and a face red from exertion. He stared at Pedro.

"Are you travelling on this bird, buddy?"

"No."

"Well I am."

"So, I understand."

"Then you should also understand that this model has two engines and both of them must be in full working order and running nice and smooth before we lift off."

"I would think so."

'Yeah." Bert spat on the dry earth. "Right now, there's a small problem with one engine."

"How small?"

With exaggerated patience, the pilot said, "To run, engines need oil."

"Got it."

"One engine is not getting oil because there's a leak. That makes it compromised. I would even say, inoperative."

Pedro was getting tired of this. "Enough with the sarcasm. Can you fix it?"

Bert blinked. "I'm trying," he said. "It needs a washer and a pin to keep the washer in place. I have the washer but no pin."

"That's all?"

"That's all, and if there was a 'Pep Boys' round the corner, everything would be fine, but there ain't."

"How big is the pin?"

"Here, take a look."

Sacrificing his expensive slacks, Pedro knelt by Bert and peered up at the innards. "Look left," said Bert. "That one's fine. But the one on the right is done, shot."

Pedro could see this was the case. "How could that happen?"

"Old age," said Bert. "Plumb wore out. This piece of junk is almost as old as I am, and some of my own components are pretty creaky if you want the truth."

Tell me about it, thought Pedro. He said, "I'm paying a lot of money for this piece of junk, as you call it. I think I have a right to expect it would work."

Bert looked pityingly at him. "You're not an engineer, are you."

"I'm in investment."

"That figures. An engineer would know that stuff always happens."

Pedro was looking at the pin, the good one. "Hang on a minute."

He scrambled through the undergrowth back to his car, a brand new Infiniti G90. It was his wife's but she was out of town and he liked to steal it sometimes because it was fun to drive. In the glovebox she kept various female necessities. He rummaged around, found what he was looking for and came back. He showed it to Bert who peered suspiciously.

"A bobby pin?"

"It happens to be the same size as the one that's missing. A bit longer in fact, but you could twist the end over."

Bert took it, fiddled with pliers and threaded it into its appointed place just upstream of the sump. It fitted perfectly.

He climbed into the cockpit and gunned the engines, first one and then the other. Both fired first time. He revved them up and ran them for a minute, then dialled them back to 'idle.' He nodded at Pedro.

Pedro looked at his watch. It was five minutes past departure time. Late, but not too late. No need to abort.

Bert wiped his oily hands on a rag and leaned out of the cockpit. The troopers were lined up and watching anxiously. He gave a little bow.

"Your carriage awaits, gentlemen." There was a ragged cheer and they started boarding. He flourished his U.S. Air Force cap, then jammed it back on his head.

"Er," said Pedro.

"What now?" barked Bert, moustache twitching.

"Are you planning to wear that cap?"

"Sure am."

"It's just that it might provoke an international incident."

"How?"

"We're going to land on Cuban soil. This isn't a U.S. government exercise but even so, if you wear that hat it might be interpreted as one by Cuba."

Bert looked thoughtful, his tiny blue eyes screwed up in his red face. "Thing is, I always wear this hat. It's a lucky hat."

"But this time, you should leave it behind."

Bert eyed him and shook his head. "No hat, no trip."

Pedro knew when to back down.

Everyone was now on board. Pedro stood watching along with one disappointed soldier, Felipe. Felipe had been assigned to stay behind at the camp to monitor communications and generally keep watch. They had drawn lots and Felipe got the short straw.

They were about to close the door and raise the ramp when Bert glanced out the cockpit window.

"Last call," he shouted at Pedro over the engine noise.

Pedro smiled and shook his head.

"Don't trust that bobby pin?" asked Bert.

Pedro shrugged, stepped forward, climbed the short ramp and hopped into the cabin. *Once in a while you make a dumb decision*, he thought. His wife would divorce him if she knew, but she wouldn't be back for a couple of days and this excursion would only last six hours if it went well. If it didn't . . . he preferred not to think about that. The co-pilot's seat opposite Bert was empty so he went forward and sat in it, to good natured cheers from the other passengers. He strapped himself in. The engine noise was deafening. Bert pointed to headphones and Pedro put them on.

The helicopter rose three thousand feet and turned south before accelerating to its cruising speed.

"We're off," Bert's voice crackled in the headphones.

Pedro stared out of the window. It was disconcerting to be moving at speed through total darkness. It was a moonless night as predicted so, although there were no clouds, the sky was black and he could see nothing. He wondered how they were navigating. He glanced at Bert who, after checking gauges and trimming the vehicle, was sitting with his hands lightly on the controls.

"How do you know where to go?"

"Part dead-reckoning, part city lights," Bert explained.

"Dead reckoning?"

"Yes. I know the direction to fly and because there's very little wind, I can assume that by flying at a steady speed in a given direction for a fixed time, I'll arrive at a certain point."

"What about city lights? I don't see any."

"You won't see Miami because we're being careful to keep out of commercial airspace. We don't want to attract attention, for obvious reasons. We didn't file a flight plan."

"What will be your markers, then?"

"In an hour we should see Key West on our left. At that point we'll change course to 225 degrees and head towards Cancun."

Pedro said, "You make it sound easy."

"It's not. It will get a bit tricky after that because we have to know where to change course again. Cuban cities don't have lights anywhere near as powerful as those in the States. Our last marker will be Havana but, again, we don't want to get too close for fear of being detected."

"So what will you do?"

"The new moon will have risen over Cuba by then. It will provide a little light. We'll use that to pick up the coastline at the eastern tip of Cuba near Pinar del Rio. Coastlines are very helpful, as Allied bombers found in the Second World War when they used them as markers during raids on Germany. We'll follow the coast for a while and then hope to spot the Cuban island known in pre-Castro days as

Isla de Pinos. The capital Nueva Gerona will be our reference. Then we'll be getting warm."

All this made Pedro feel reasonably confident. Bert sounded as if he had tackled tougher navigational challenges in his long career.

"How will you navigate the final leg?"

Bert shrugged. For the first time, he looked less confident. "That'll be the hard part."

"Why?"

"After Nueva Gerona there are no more markers. It will be dead reckoning from there on."

"Just for a short distance?"

"Yeah but it's a small island. Easy to miss."

"What happens if we do miss?"

"Then we're in trouble. Every pilot remembers what happened to Amelia Earhart."

Pedro looked puzzled.

"Amelia was flying round the world with a co-pilot. After leaving New Guinea they flew towards Howland Island, an uninhabited coral island. It had a rough airstrip where she planned to refuel with the help of a US Coastguard ship. Howland is about the same size as where we are going."

"What happened?"

"Nobody knows. Her plane was never seen again. Radio requests indicated that it got within a hundred miles of the island but due to radio incompatibility between the ship and the plane, the plane was unable to receive directions."

"So they were lost?"

He nodded. "It probably missed the island, ran out of gas and crashed in the sea."

"Which is what could happen to us?"

"You got it!"

Pedro tried to smile. "Thanks for the reassurance."

45

Bruno looked up at the sky. "It'll be dark soon."

I looked at my watch. Six thirty. The little boat was chugging south through a light swell, out of sight of land. It felt very lonely.

An hour later it was completely dark. Then a small pinprick of light in the gloom ahead betrayed the presence of the island.

I felt my heart leap. Until then I think I had subconsciously avoided considering what could go wrong with a very risky plan but now the rubber was about to hit the road – or the beach.

I glanced at Sinbad who was at the wheel. His weather-beaten face was expressionless, as if he did this sort of thing every day. Well, perhaps he did. He was in the people smuggling game. At least he was unlikely to lose his nerve.

I checked the time again. It was still thirty minutes before zero hour. "How long will it take to reach shore?" I asked.

"About twenty minutes."

"Let's pause out here before going in. I want to hit the shore at zero minus five. It will take a few minutes to get from the shore to the office which is where we need to be."

Sinbad nodded and throttled back the engine. There was silence except for the water slapping the vessel's wooden sides.

I pulled out my map. "Let's go over this one more time."

Bruno produced a small flashlight and shone it on the much-folded page. I tapped it with my pencil.

"There's a strip of beach here, at the north-west tip of the island. We'll land there. It's not close to buildings so we shouldn't be spotted. Bruno and I will go ashore."

Bruno nodded. "Armed, right?"

"Of course. Machine guns and pistols plus an extra magazine for each."

"Only one extra?"

I nodded. "The weapons are for self defence. We're not planning a shooting war. If it does come to that we're probably done for."

He looked disappointed, but nodded.

I turned to Sinbad. "As soon as you've dropped

us off, pull out a hundred yards from the shoreline and wait. We'll flash you a signal when we're ready to leave – three short flashes and one long, V for victory – and you come in ASAP and pick us up."

Sinbad frowned. "What is ASAP?"

"It means don't screw around, get here immediately. Or sooner!"

He laughed. "ASAP. That's good. I learn each day better English."

"Not better, just more."

"Okay."

"Next, Bruno, you and I make our way to the Administration Office. It's situated on the north tip of the island, close to where we are landing. Keys to the yard and to the prison cells should be there. We shall restrain the personnel and take the keys."

"You make it sound easy."

"I don't mean to. We're only part of the plan. Hopefully the helicopter will arrive just as we break into the office. Those guys have to be on time and do their stuff. Their job is to land and neutralise the garrison. Otherwise we shall be heavily outnumbered and if that happens, frankly, we're cooked."

Bruno said: "That would also be our last chance to abort the project: no helicopter, no attack?"

I shook my head. "There's no 'abort', only Plan B."

"Which is?"

"Go into the office, hold up the occupants, ask

them nicely to hand over the keys. That's why I have a silenced pistol – to avoid alerting the garrison. I shall shoot them one by one until they comply."

He already knew all this as I had made it clear before, so I was irritated with him. Our eyes met and he gave a half smile. "Okay professor, whatever you say."

As the clock ticked down, Sinbad nudged the boat inshore on minimum power. Ten feet from land its keel bumped on the sandy bottom.

"Jump," he said. "Good luck!"

We scrambled through the water, weapons at shoulder height.

Enough light spilled from the window of the office to make the sandy ground visible. We reached the office unseen and paused outside the door to listen.

I could hear voices – too many voices for comfort. It sounded like several people inside. I checked my watch again. Zero hour exactly. I glanced at the sky. If the helicopter was within several miles we should hear the noise of its rotors but there was no sound.

"Let's go," I muttered. I gently turned the door-knob, then threw the door open.

There were three people inside, sitting around a metal desk. Their faces were a study, changing instantly from surprise to alarm.

One of them caught my attention immediately. His smart uniform and well groomed hair made him look entirely out of place. The thin lips and pointed black beard gave him an air of authority. But even he was nonplussed as he saw my pistol and the machine gun Bruno was levelling at the group.

His companions were shabbier, both wearing grubby unpressed khakis – one was an older man, the other more junior. The elder was maybe fifty, stout and red-faced, the body flabby, his sullen face sporting a day's stubble. The younger, in his twenties, was slimmer and more athletic looking.

I scanned the room looking for keys and saw what I wanted almost immediately, on a board on the wall. Keys on numbered hooks, like a cheap hotel.

"Where's Feaver?" I snapped at the well-dressed man.

A look of comprehension spread over his face. He shook his head with a half smile. I was pretty sure who he was. It might be difficult to bully him into giving up a key.

He looked me up and down. "American? I confess I didn't expect you quite so soon."

I ignored him and motioned Bruno to move round the desk, nearer the keys.

"Talk Spanish to the fat one," I said. "Make it

clear that unless he gives you Kon's key you'll shoot him."

He nodded and spoke quickly, accompanied by a menacing thrust of the machine gun, the tip of the barrel pushed under the man's chin. It had the desired effect. Bruno lifted a key from its hook with a flourish and nodded at me.

The young guard grabbed a telephone on the desk. Before either of us could react, he put his mouth close to the instrument and shouted "Ayuda!" which, even to my linguistically challenged brain, was a cry for help. Either he was made of sterner stuff or else was more foolhardy than his companion.

Bruno swung the Kalashnikov and hit the young man hard in the face. He dropped the 'phone but the damage was done.

It was the worst thing that could have happened. Now we could expect the garrison to arrive at any moment. We had a key, hopefully the right one, but we were still only at the beginning of our mission and already it was going wrong. I listened again for the helicopter, but there was nothing.

The island's barracks were a quarter of a mile to the south. One or more guards would arrive in moments.

Bruno said "I'll go find Kon. You stay here." He

grabbed the fat guard and propelled him towards the door.

I nodded. It made sense for Bruno to take him. The guard seemed cowed but even so, language issues would make it hard for me to get through to him. They left the hut and disappeared into the darkness.

I moved to where I could cover both remaining Cubans. There was an awkward silence.

"You don't look like the kind of person who would fire that weapon," said the uniformed man in accented but correct English.

I knew what he meant. I'm an accountant, not a gunman and although I'm reasonably fit I've been told I look studious, not athletic.

There was a framed picture of Fidel Castro on the wall. It seemed a suitable target. I pointed the Ruger at the picture and fired a single shot.

The glass shattered. The picture wavered on its hook and fell to the floor with a clatter. It was the famous one of El Comandante as a bearded young soldier in fatigues and backpack, evoking early days in the hills of the Sierra Maestre. It depicted the young revolutionary hero before his Marxist views were revealed and his political rivals began to disappear or die, one by one.

I nodded at him. "You're right, it's not my style. But desperate times . . . "

The shot, though silenced, had shaken the air in the small room. He might not have been frightened, but he was definitely surprised.

"It's a full clip," I said. "There's twelve rounds left. Don't make me use them."

He frowned. "You're being absurd. The guards will be here in a moment." No humour now. He was right. The attempt to find Kon was starting to seem hopeless. I pointed the gun at his midriff.

"You're a long way from home," I suggested.

He nodded. "As you said, desperate times."

"Is that why you kidnapped Sanchez Madera?" I asked.

It was clear from his expression that I had guessed his identity.

"What do you know about that?"

"We know everything we need to know about you," I said.

"Who are you?"

"My name is Oliver Steele. We have a file of information including a section detailing your transactions with the Russian Embassy."

"Ridiculous lies."

I shook my head. "We also know you're holding Martin Sanchez Madera. Unless he is released, your file will be handed to the Ministry of the Interior. That will be the end of your career, and possibly even your life. At the very least you'll have to get used to a bug-infested cell with a hole in the floor."

"What nonsense."

"You will not be the first person who rubbed the Castros the wrong way and paid a heavy price. Remember General Ochoa."

Cruz scowled. In 1989 the war hero Armando Ochoa had been convicted of importing several tons of cocaine from Colombia for shipment to the United States. He was demoted, tried and shot but there was a widely-held suspicion that the drug trafficking had been organised with Fidel's approval as part of his programme to generate hard currency.

"You forget something," he said. "I have arrested the compiler of that file. I know where the file is. A young woman staying at the Nacional Hotel will shortly be relieved of it and she too will be in my custody."

I had not expected that and my face must have shown my concern. He laughed. "Americans shouldn't interfere in Cuban politics. They should mind their own business."

Just then I heard the long awaited thudding of helicopter rotors in the sky, getting closer. Cruz's eyes widened. To say I was relieved is a huge understatement.

"Friends of mine," I said casually. The noise swelled to a roar. I ducked outside and watched as the helicopter descended onto what was basically a large empty space, dry and sandy. A spotlight mounted on its belly shone down, illuminating the ground. Huge clouds of dust flew up.

The machine settled slowly on its skids and came to rest. The door opened and one after another the brigadistas vaulted out, weapons ready.

Beyond the clearing, I could see other figures approaching from the south, presumably members of the garrison. As best I could see they were carrying handguns but not rifles.

Shots were fired and a Cuban guard fell. More guards turned or ran to one side or the other, away from the line of fire.

In the spotlight I could see at the same time the forms of Bruno and the gaoler. They had stopped at a small box-shaped structure and were leaning over it.

The Florida commandos were spreading out. Several confronted the approaching guards. Others joined Bruno, crowding round the 'box' which he and the guard had unlocked, loosening the lid and opening it. Bullets continued to fly but while the commandos provided covering fire, Bruno and a helper reached in and lifted out a body. They half dragged, half carried the limp form back towards the hut.

I joined them there. In the commotion, the two

Cubans – Cruz and the young guard – had disappeared.

We deposited Kon in a chair and he eyed us blearily. His clothing was filthy, several days growth of beard adorned his stained face and he was about one tenth conscious but he mustered the ghost of a smile.

"Water." His lips formed the outline of the word. Pedro Macias found a cup, filled it from the tap and held it to his lips. He soaked a rag in more water and wiped Kon's face.

Then he turned to me. "What now?"

"Good question," I said.

46

THE GUNFIRE WAS INTENSIFYING. The helicopter had landed about a hundred yards south of the hut and the garrison was another hundred yards south of that. For the moment we were away from the field of fire but around the 'copter a full-on battle was raging. The Black Eagles were at a disadvantage because the floodlights surrounding the pad were shining full in their faces but they were giving as good as they got.

Amid the noise I tried to keep calm and take stock. I had sensed from Cruz's manner that he was expecting us, just not so soon. I didn't know how that happened but it explained the readiness of his troops. Some shooting injuries were probable for our side and there was an added danger – the helicopter was at risk of being immobilised. One stray bullet in the wrong place would do it.

If that happened, Bruno and I and Kon might sneak away by boat but our brigadistas would be in real trouble. They would be forced to wait until Cuban reinforcements arrived from the mainland to arrest them or shoot them.

I wouldn't give much for our troops' chances if that happened, even if their lives were spared. After the Bay of Pigs in 1961, when fifteen hundred Cuban-American troops landed just twenty miles north of here in a disastrously botched invasion, several hundred were killed or executed later. Eleven hundred were put on trial and sentenced to thirty years in prison. Castro demanded a price of five hundred heavy agricultural tractors for their release. Negotiations dragged on for two years, interrupted by the Cuban missile crisis in 1962. Finally, with the help of CIA chief Allen Dulles and a raft of top diplomats, the eleven hundred were returned to the United States in exchange for food and medical supplies, Castro wringing every last drop of public relations value from the affair.

It was safe to say that this time there would be no U.S. diplomats pulling for us, quite the opposite. Uncle Sam wouldn't touch our unsanctioned invasion with a very long pole, so we had to get it right ourselves.

"We need a flanking movement," I said. I hustled Bruno and Pedro along with me and we made off to the left, which was eastwards.

"Wha lies this way?" asked Pedro. He had scrounged an AK47 from somewhere, presumably there were weapons on the 'copter. He also had a heavy looking canvas bag slung over his shoulder.

"Not much, just beach. What's in the bag?"

"Grenades. Thought they might come in handy. What's the plan?"

"If we sprint south along the beach for a couple of hundred yards we should come to the garrison building. We can move inland and attack them from the side. Collapse of unsuspecting parties."

Pedro said nothing. We reached the sand, only to find that it was high tide and the beach was barely two feet wide. We slogged onwards through wet sand and lapping surf, going slower and slower. After a few minutes Pedro asked, "Shouldn't we be turning inland now?"

It was too dark to see anything. I used my flashlight but its strength was pathetic, petering out in the inky darkness, the battery running low. I had to admit I was lost. So I said the only thing a leader could say. "Exactly. In we go!"

We were navigating by dead reckoning again but this time on the ground instead of in the air. We almost knocked heads with a solid brick building and pulled up short.

"Are we there?" hissed Pedro.

I squandered some precious flashlight power. The building didn't look right. No windows, no lights. A single padlocked door and, on it, a sign – the skull and crossbones of all things. It took a moment, then the penny dropped.

"This isn't the garrison, it's the generating station."

"We're too far south," said Bruno.

"Let's double back," Pedro said.

I was about to agree without further comment. Whoever said, 'Never apologise, never explain!' had a point. Then a thought struck me.

"Hold on," I said. "We need a diversion, don't we?"

"Well... yeah."

"I know you're dying to use those pineapples, or at least one of them."

Pedro pulled a murderous looking device from his bag. "An M67 fragmentation grenade, as used in Vietnam and Afghanistan. Very reliable." He started to reach for the pin.

"Hold on a moment. How far does the explosion reach when one of those goes off?"

He sounded surprised. "Don't know. In the movies they just throw them and duck. Seems to work."

Bruno said, "If you don't mind, I'm going to start running." He began to move away.

Pedro laughed. "I have a pretty strong arm. But first I'm going to break down that door."

He jemmied the padlock and pushed the door ajar. Then we retreated until Pedro said, "About here should do it."

He pulled the pin and we threw ourselves down on the damp sand. I held my breath but he was as good as his word. He threw the grenade with a graceful lob and it sailed through the building's open door. I had barely counted to three when it detonated. The shock was huge, battering our eardrums. A vivid flash lit the sky. Simultaneously, every light on the island went out.

The sound of gunfire stopped briefly. Then it began again, but more limited. I thought I knew what was happening. The Black Eagles were using their searchlights, but the defending troops had no such light to guide their aim. The advantage had swung in favour of the attackers.

The generating station was now burning vigorously, so visibility near us, though not great, was better than elsewhere. "One more thing," I said, remembering my map. "Do you have more grenades?"

"Sure."

"There's another structure about fifty feet from the generating station that deserves your attention."

"Namely?"

"The fuel store."

"Fuel as in?"

"Gasoline."

I couldn't see Pedro's face but I think he smiled.

By the flames from the generating station we could make out two massive gasoline tanks mounted side by side on concrete blocks.

"Our targets," I said. "I don't know if a grenade will set them off but it's worth a try."

One grenade lobbed by Pedro did the trick, so the try was more than worth it. When the tanks erupted, the entire island seemed to catch fire.

Most of the heart seemed to go out of the defending troops after that. One after another they put down their arms and raised their hands.

47

"ARE YOU HURT?" I asked Luis.

His fatigues were spattered with dust and there was a streak of blood on his right arm.

He laughed. "Just a graze." He almost seemed proud of it.

I stood talking to Luis and Pedro near the helicopter. Pedro looked urbane but muddied. He was still wearing the street clothes in which he left Miami earlier in the day.

"First things first," I said. "The best place for Kon is on the 'copter. Get him to Florida and find him some medical attention."

"What about the brigadistas?" asked Luis. A few sporadic shots were still coming from the direction of the barracks.

"Have them keep the garrison pinned down," I

said. "The important thing is, where are Hector Cruz and his young friend?"

"Is that important?" asked Bruno.

"Very much so. I'll explain later."

I remembered a feature on my map of the island. "I may know where they are." I signalled to Luis. "Come with me. Bring a flashlight."

We walked over to the west coast of the island, a hundred yards south of where Sinbad had deposited us. A knot of palm trees loomed, pale in Luis's flashlight.

"Shine it around," I said.

"What are we looking for?"

"I'm not sure. But the map suggested a hiding place or sanctuary of some kind. I'm not sure what. A concrete hut, maybe?"

There was no hut. But as Luis played his flashlight over the sandy ground I noticed a raised area about the size of a manhole or trapdoor. I rooted in the sand with my foot and felt a hard edge. Brushing away the sand, I exposed a manhole cover. We prised it open to reveal a vertical shaft with metal rungs let into the side. I weighed the idea of climbing down but had second thoughts.

Instead, I raised my voice, "Cruz, you have two choices. Number one: come up and we can talk things over."

There was silence from below.

"Last call," I said.

Then, "What is the second choice?" His voice.

"I have an AK47 here. It has a thirty round magazine. It's a little old fashioned but even an amateur like me can fire five rounds a second, which is plenty."

"Plenty for what?"

"On the count of three, I shall start firing into your tunnel. One shot at a time. I don't know where the bullets will go but sooner or later I shall hit you. I may kill you or I may just part your hair. If the latter, I shall fire again. It's up to you."

"That is inhuman."

"Yep. Like your treatment of my friend, Kon Feaver."

On the count of two, Cruz's face appeared, smeared with dirt. He climbed awkwardly out of the hole.

"Keep him covered," I told Luis.

By now the firefight was over. The island garrison had only consisted of six guards. Besides being outnumbered, the Cubans had been demoralised from the start by the unexpected onslaught. The Florida commandos had brought plastic ties for use as handcuffs and we herded the guards into their own cell block, one man to a cell.

That done, Luis grinned and asked, "What now?"

"You've accomplished the mission, well done. If

Bert can get that machine airborne again you can head home, with Kon on board."

"What about you and Bruno?"

"We're going back to Cuba by boat and Señor Cruz is coming with us."

The pale-faced policeman, hands fastened behind him, his uniform badly dirtied, scowled.

I shook hands with Luis and Pedro. "Wait until we are at sea, just to be safe. Then you can take off."

We made our way down to our embarkation point and flashed a signal and moments later Sinbad drew up in the boat.

"You didn't say there would be fireworks," he said drily.

"We weren't sure ourselves."

"Things went okay?"

"I'd say so." I indicated Cruz. "We have a passenger."

Sinbad noticed the handcuffs. "I'll make him comfortable."

"Not too comfortable," I said.

On the boat back I sat opposite Cruz.

"Why are you holding me?" he growled.

"You'll see. You're going to help us out with something."

"Never."

"I think so. When we land we're going to take you somewhere safe. Then there will be a prisoner exchange."

"I don't understand."

"There are a couple of people whose safety I'm holding you accountable for. One is Martin Sanchez Madera. The other is his wife."

"Worthless, both of them."

"In your eyes, perhaps."

"They have betrayed the Revolution."

I sighed. "I'm pretty tired of hearing that phrase. How would you describe your own behaviour?"

"I support the government and constitution of Cuba."

"Sure you do, for now. What about when Raul steps down?"

"Cuba will need leadership. I shall provide it."

"By force?"

"If necessary. It will be for the good of the people."

"As defined by you."

He shrugged.

I changed the subject. I had been asking myself where Cruz would keep his money – the funds he earned from the deal with his pal at the Russian embassy.

Not in Cuba obviously, he would go offshore. Probably somewhere nearby. The Bahamas, Belize,

Panama and the Caymans were all handy if a physical visit was necessary.

Grand Cayman was nearest, nestling in the Caribbean just south of Cuba. From a language point of view Spanish-speaking Panama might be better. But the Caymans were more accessible from Cruz's southern headquarters. I took a chance.

I smiled at Cruz.

"I know about your Cayman account," I said.

The look on his face told me I had guessed right.

"I also know the account number," I said. That wasn't true, I just wanted to scare him.

48

CALEB WAS FEELING good as he caught the bus into Havana and walked the last few blocks to Café Hola for the group's second performance.

The warm glow he experienced the night before had surprised him. It had been ages since he had been on stage jamming with friends and he had forgotten the feeling of well-being, a buzz that stayed with you afterwards and made everything in your life – colours, tastes, emotions – seem just a little better.

He knew something was wrong when he saw the hall was locked and unlit. A notice scrawled on a sheet of paper taped to the door simply said 'Closed.'

He called Pepe on the number he had for him and got a recording telling him to leave a message.

"Pepe, it's Caleb. What's up? Call me." But he had

an empty feeling in his stomach. He didn't really expect to hear back. It had all been too good to be true.

He did not feel like taking this setback meekly so, next morning, he went to the office where Pepe had interviewed him.

He walked straight in, anger and disappointment welling up in his chest. The big break had seemed so close.

Pepe was there. He looked surprised and embarrassed to see Caleb. "Oh, hi!"

Caleb nodded. "What's the story? The concert went well, so why is the hall deserted now?"

Pepe shrugged. "Circumstances beyond my control, my friend."

"That may be, but I'd still like to know why."

Pepe's look was borderline hostile. He would clearly have preferred not to answer but the grizzled singer planted himself in front of the young man and glared.

Pepe sighed. "If you must know, my investor is cooling off."

"Who is this investor?"

"That's none of your business. But he's a big casino owner based in Las Vegas."

"Why did he back out?"

"He said he had other priorities." Pepe was reading his mail, pointedly ignoring Caleb.

Caleb resented the rudeness. He was angry and disappointed at seeing his future dissolve and collapse before his eyes. He moved forward without thinking, grasped the young man by his shirt collar and shook him.

Pepe recoiled, astonished, and pulled free, adjusting his shirt.

"I told you the truth. If you must know, I used the last of the American's money to pay you. I had an email from him a few hours later, backing out. His marketing people told him the Cuban thing was oversold, whatever that means. He's clearly not short of funds, but when all's said and done he can invest wherever he wants. I guess that's just not in Cuba."

Caleb realised for the first time that Pepe had been hurt as much as he had himself. The young man probably expected to make a big killing, offshore funds and all, and had felt the cold corporate decision just as much of a body blow as Caleb. A brief look of commiseration passed between the two.

Caleb shrugged, nodded and turned to leave. Pepe sat gazing morosely into space. A small timer scrabbling to make it in the teeth of Yanqui capitalism.

He's young, he'll bounce back, thought Caleb morosely. Not like me with the clock ticking. A few miserable Cuban pesos from shining shoes were his own best hope.

49

I<small>T WAS</small> three in the morning when Sinbad delivered us back to the beach where he had picked us up.

"You did us proud," I said. I shook the grizzled sailor's hand.

His parchment face split in a grin. "Just another job. More fun than most, to be honest. And I really don't like that guy." He gestured towards Cruz.

"Where are you headed next?" I asked.

"I have a run from Pinar del Rio."

"To Florida?"

"To Cancun."

"Cancun?" I was surprised. The Mexican resort was 150 miles from the western coastline of Cuba.

He nodded. "It's an alternative to Florida as an exit route. From Cancun the refugees go to a safe house nearby. From there they are leaked in little groups of three or four to Nuevo Laredo on the Mexican side of the U.S. border. There they merge in with the hundreds who cross the border from Nuevo Laredo to Laredo, Texas to work every day."

He laughed. "They are warned to say as little as possible because the Cuban accent is very different from the Mexican and would give them away."

"Aren't they deported when they get to the U.S.A?"

He shook his head. "Once they reach the United States they can claim asylum under the Cuban American Adjustment Act."

I understood. That was the so-called 'Wet Foot-Dry Foot' rule that allowed Cubans, but nobody else, the right to stay in the United States when they set foot on U.S. soil.

"Well good luck, and thanks."

Bruno's van was in the woods where we had left it.

"What are your plans for me?" Cruz asked.

I ignored the question. His manner was sullen. He was unused to not being in control and I almost sympathised but I wasn't going to give him any leeway. As long as he was alive he was dangerous.

I looked around and found a grubby sack about two feet across.

"Sorry if this is awkward," I said. I pulled it over

his head and fastened it with twine. He was clearly uncomfortable, with restricted breathing and plastic ties biting into his wrists but it was important that he not know where we were taking him.

I bundled him, hooded and tied, into the back of the van and sat beside him with my pistol in his ribs. I had given Bruno his driving instructions out of earshot of Cruz and in a while we reached our destination.

Teresita's parents' home was simple but clean, consisting of two rooms and a screened off area that served as a bathroom. The only kitchen was a stove outside on the porch with a sheet of corrugated iron overhead against sun and rain. Alongside it was an old refrigerator, once white, now stained with rust. Across the back yard was a toilet in a wooden outhouse.

I led Cruz into the bedroom and sat him on the bed. Before removing the sack, I drew the curtains across the only window. The thin material admitted light but made it impossible for him to see out.

"Where are we?" he muttered.

"Never mind. But two things. First, this place is remote. Nobody can hear you. Second, it's somewhere your friends would never think to look. So you are completely alone."

"What is the point of all this?"

"Here's what's going to happen: First you are going to call your office and tell your associates to release Sanchez Madera and his wife."

He scowled. "I don't know where they are."

"That's not my problem. Until I hear they are safe, you will remain without food or water. And your handcuffs, which I see are causing you some discomfort, will not be loosened. If necessary, you will die."

I called Bruno in.

"Bruno will make calls for you, using his mobile phone. I don't know how good phone tracing technology is in Cuba but we're going to put you in the van with that bag over your head, and drive a few miles, so your calls will come from a remote place and be untraceable. Then we'll bring you back."

I could see the gears clicking in his mind as he tried to find a way of gaming the plan.

"One last thing," I said. "You may be thinking you can re-arrest Sanchez Madera and his wife later on. Remember we still have your file, with full details of how you cheated the state. It has been photocopied and a copy sent to my associates in Florida."

I was winging it there because I hadn't yet spoken to Mimi in Havana, but I was relying on her to do that. I went on, "I realise that in a year or two you will make your political move. Personally, I think you would be a disaster for Cuba but I'll leave that to Sanchez Madera and others to handle. Once the Castros are both gone, the information in your file will be moot but until then it's an unanswerable weapon against you."

His facial expression was one of rage which told me my plan was right on the money.

I nodded at Bruno. "Ready?"

50

I CALLED MIMI IN HAVANA. "Kon is safe."

"Thank God."

I warned her about what Cruz had threatened – that he would capture her and recover the incriminating file.

I expected her to sound scared but all she said was, "Thanks, I'll be careful."

"It's very serious," I said.

"I said I'll be careful."

I got a brief glimpse of the girl who by the age of twenty-five had gone from being a secretary in Liverpool to a Playboy centrefold, to the wife of a billionaire.

"About the file," I said. "That dossier is our leverage against Cruz. If he retrieves it, he could re-arrest Sanchez Madera and his wife and have them tossed in jail or killed. You need to make a copy."

"I'll find a copier somewhere."

"Good plan."

"What will you do with yourself?" Mimi asked. "Get out fast is my advice."

"Or lie very low. I'll work something out."

"Okay, I'll handle the copying."

When I put the phone down, Bruno and I looked at each other.

"She must be quite something," said Bruno.

"She is," I said.

"So what next?"

"Well, we've achieved our main goal. Kon should be back in Florida by now."

Bruno shook his head. "I'm amazed we got home alive."

"Me too. I think we've also taken care of Sanchez Madera and his wife."

"Yeah. Under pressure, Cruz gave instructions to his people to set them free in Santa Clara."

"I certainly hope so. There's still a doubt in my mind."

"What could go wrong?"

"I don't know. But I shan't relax until I've met

them face to face and heard from their own lips that they are okay."

Bruno nodded. "Cruz made it clear that Sanchez Madera was to phone me when they were free."

"Let's wait and see if that happens."

"What do we do with Cruz?" he asked.

"We'll take him to Santa Clara with us."

"He's not exactly a congenial travel companion."

"He's a miserable bugger," I said. "But we'll put the bag over his head again if he becomes a nuisance."

Bruno laughed. "Okay."

We hit the road again. Bruno drove while I sat in the back with Cruz. I did keep the bag on his head. I didn't want him to know where we had been. He was clearly a vindictive character and if he ever got the chance he would take revenge on anyone he could find, including Teresita.

Bruno's phone rang as we were driving. He spoke briefly, then passed it to me. It was Sanchez Madera.

"Hi Martin," I said. "Are you okay?"

"I'm fine. I don't know what you did but Sylvia and I were released half an hour ago. Thank you!"

"Where are you now?"

"In the town square of Santa Clara. They drove us there and dumped us without money or possessions. Luckily, Sylvia has a cousin nearby who came and gave us money."

"Good, we need to talk. We're on our way to Santa Clara – we should be with you in an hour. Where shall we meet?"

"How about the main square, Parque Vidal? It's a fine day. We'll be sitting on a bench in front of the statue of Marta Abreu de Estévez, a local benefactress."

"Pre-revolutionary?"

"Of course."

Sure enough, Martin and his wife were there when we arrived. The young Cuban shook me warmly by the hand.

He listened as I explained how we had secured his release. I also explained about the dossier.

"Where is it now?" he asked.

"Mimi has it in Havana."

"That's good. But we may have another problem."

"Yes?"

"Stanley Rothman."

"Rothman the casino owner? Where does he fit into the picture?"

"When the Russian money dried up, Cruz put out feelers in search of finance. He wangled an introduction to Rothman and they saw that their interests coincided. But I think that relationship may be doomed to fail."

"Why?"

"Rothman will realise Cruz is compromised now that the dossier is in our hands."

"If he finds out."

"Which he will, sooner or later."

Sanchez Madera went on. "Rothman is as sharp a piece of work as you'll find north *or* south of the Florida Straits. If you were he, what would be your next step?"

"I would look for another Cuban contact, someone who is not as vulnerable as Cruz."

Sanchez Madera nodded. "And you would find one. I love my compatriots but they are not saints. Someone will step up."

"You think so?"

"Yeah. Like Cruz they will be looking ahead, anticipating the post-Castro era."

"Well that's a problem for another day," I said. "Right now, I plan to spend some time lying on the beach with Kathy at a luxury hotel on Cayo Santa Maria."

51

MIMI WENT DOWNSTAIRS to the Hotel Nacional restaurant.

The buffet was huge. There was ham, steak, waffles, eggs in every form, smoked salmon, porridge, various kinds of cheese and fresh rolls, bagels and croissants. Any shortages in Cuba had not penetrated the privileged halls of the Nacional. The monthly wage of a state employee would barely cover the cost of Mimi's breakfast.

She helped herself to waffles and maple syrup, which she took back to her table overlooking green lawns and the hotel pool. By her second cup of coffee, she had a plan.

. . .

Back in her room she retrieved the Cruz file, then returned to the lobby and followed a sign to the business office on the second floor.

A young woman behind the desk, dark-haired and carefully made up, smiled. "How can I help?"

"I need to copy some papers," she said.

"Of course." The woman saw the envelope and held out her hand.

"I mean, I'd like to copy them myself."

The woman looked surprised. "I can do it."

"No, I really prefer to do it, the contents are very confidential."

A shadow passed over the woman's brow. "We have a policy. The cost is reasonable. How many pages are there?"

She's pretty, thought Mimi, but she's the kind who follows orders. She smiled and left, making her excuses.

She went back to her room and called Bruno.

"Hola!"

"Bruno, listen, is there a copying machine in your office?"

"No."

"That's a pity." She explained the situation.

"But there is a computer printer that makes copies."

"That will do."

"It's brand new. In fact, it's still in the box from Japan. I have a buyer for it."

"This is an emergency, Bruno. If it costs you a sale we'll make it up to you."

He didn't sound happy but he told her how to get to his office. To enter the building she would need a key from the cleaner who lived nearby.

"Be sure to lock the door when you leave," he said. "The stuff in that house is worth its weight in gold. My livelihood is in there."

"Don't worry."

She studied the map. His office was a long walk across town, a walk she didn't feel like braving. She would take a cab.

As she spoke to the bell captain, she did not notice a man standing at the far end of the lobby watching her. He was well-groomed, a tanned face contrasting with his pale coloured suit. He could have been a businessman or an attorney. As she climbed into her taxi, he moved forward and got into a private car waiting nearby. It was a plain white Lada, not one of the decorative old vehicles so appealing to tourists.

When Mimi got down near Bruno's house, the man stopped a block further on, then followed her on foot as she retrieved the key from the cleaner and let herself in.

She found the printer in its shiny box but then

had to assemble it and connect it to the electrical supply. She was not mechanically minded so it was a laborious task, but she finally succeeded. By sliding the pages into a hopper on the machine, she was able to do the job in one pass, copying both sides, rather than having to stand and feed the pages one by one. So she felt successful as she let herself out of the house clutching a large envelope.

She strolled through the narrow streets, charming despite their weather-beaten appearance. Havana had a logical street pattern, the streets at right angles making a series of blocks and by glimpsing the ocean she knew roughly where she was, so she decided to walk back to the hotel.

She had just made the decision when she felt someone at her elbow. She turned in surprise.

"Allow me, Señora."

The hand on a fawn-suited arm gripped her wrist hard. She resisted but he tightened his hold. Although not tall he was broad-chested and strong. His tanned face beneath a balding head smiled blandly but the more she struggled the closer his grip.

He waved up the Lada cruising behind him and bundled her into the back seat.

The car sped across town, not slowing until it reached upscale Vedado, an expensive area with embassies and some fine old villas. They stopped at a well-kept mansion and she was ushered through the front door into a large reception room. No expense had been spared in decorating it. Antique furniture on a stone floor strewn with expensive rugs.

A short, older man with thinning red-grey hair plastered to his scalp stood in the middle of the room.

"This is outrageous," she said. "I demand to speak to someone who speaks English."

He smiled. "I can help you there. My name is Stanley Rothman from Las Vegas, Nevada."

"The casino owner?"

He gave a little bow. "We have things to discuss but first let me relieve you of your parcel. Pedro, if you would?"

The bald man detached the envelope from her grasp and handed it to Rothman, who opened it. She watched as he leafed through the pages.

He was quite old, she thought. His hands were like claws, tendons standing out and liver spots on his wrists but his face was smooth and wrinkle-free, she suspected thanks to surgery.

"Interesting," he said after a while. "That little rat Cruz, who would have thought it?"

52

As I was talking to Martin and Sylvia in the square, a group of teenage schoolchildren were laughing and chatting on a nearby bench. They wore high-school uniform, the boys in light blue shirts and navy shorts, the girls in blue blouses, pleated skirts and white socks. One of the girls was talking animatedly on an Apple phone, an older model.

It reminded me that Bruno, my favourite black marketeer, was round the corner in the van, keeping an eye on Cruz. I said goodbye to the couple and left.

Walking down Calle Luis Estevez I passed a curious looking store containing half a dozen heavy-duty sewing machines, each on its own bench. I stopped a passer-by and asked, using sign language, what it was about. He laughed and pointed at his shoes. It was a place to mend footwear. It had been years since I'd seen a cobbler's shop in the United States, let alone one where you had to do your own sewing.

I turned onto Calle Placido. The van was still there but I sensed something amiss, a feeling confirmed when I peered through the dusty window.

To my horror I saw the unconscious Bruno slumped in the driving seat. My worst fear was confirmed when I looked in the back. It was empty.

I tried the front passenger door. It was locked. I stopped a passer-by. "Por favor. Accidente!"

I won't say I was panicking but I came close.

I tugged at the driver's door again although I knew it was locked. They say insanity is doing the same thing over and over, expecting a different result. I tried the passenger side. That door opened freely, thank God. I leaned forward to take Bruno's pulse – there was some activity but it was much weaker than it should be.

The passer-by, a grey haired man in his fifties, looked like a professional of some kind. He showed surprise but came back to the van with me. My choice turned out to be good because he immediately took my arm and walked me to a store a block away marked 'Farmacia.'

He pushed to the head of the queue and fired rapid Spanish at the woman behind the counter. A white ambulance van arrived within five minutes. Paramedics loaded the limp Bruno in and drove away. It crossed my mind to offer the grey-haired Cuban money but it seemed patronising so I didn't. He shook my hand with a smile and a bow and I never saw him again.

The paramedics said I should follow the ambulance so I drove behind it to the hospital a few blocks away. I had the presence of mind to search the back of the van before I followed Bruno's stretcher into the hospital. I found a frayed and broken yellow plastic tie on the floor. Cruz must have rubbed it to and fro against a rough surface until it parted – a floor-mounted rail supporting the seat seemed the likely candidate. To forestall embarrassing questions, I removed the tie and thrust it deep in a nearby trash can.

They wheeled Bruno into one of several glass-walled emergency wards grouped round a common area. Hospitals look and smell the same everywhere in the world.

He was treated immediately by doctors and nurses who seemed to know what they were doing. Emergency rooms in the United States tend to be overcrowded because people use them for primary care but medical treatment in Cuba is famously free.

I answered questioners and gave them Bruno's name. Then I sat and waited. After twenty minutes a young doctor in white coat, stethoscope round his neck, came out to see me.

"Your friend will live," he said. He seemed uneasy.

"What's the problem?" I asked. "Is there something I should know?"

"It is more a matter of what *you* can tell *us*."

"Meaning?"

The doctor stroked his chin. "He has a bad concussion."

"Yes?"

"He was hit hard on the head. We x-rayed the skull, he's lucky not to have a fracture."

"I imagine that is not unusual in traffic accidents," I said.

The doctor looked at me. "He was in a parked car."

I smiled at the doctor. When there's nothing you can say, it's best to keep quiet.

"How did he get there?" he asked.

I continued to smile. He sighed and went back into the ward where I saw him lift Bruno's eyelids and put the stethoscope to his chest. He wrote on the chart by the side of the bed and came out again.

"He must stay here two nights, maybe longer. What's your address?"

"The Magnolia guest house," I said. It was where Bruno and I had stayed on the way south the day before – it seemed an eternity ago. I had no reservation of course.

The doctor nodded. "A decent place." But he seemed conflicted. "I need to make a call."

I saw him use the phone. He came back.

I said, "If Bruno isn't going to be fit for visitors today, I'll go back to the hotel."

He held up a hand. "Please wait a little longer. There are some formalities."

"What formalities?" But he had turned away.

Five minutes later two men in PNR uniform arrived and approached me. "Mr. Steele?"

"Yes."

"We have a few questions."

"What sort of questions?"

"Routine questions. It's normal in a case like this. Please come."

Which was how I came to be tossed into a Cuban jail.

53

"Mr. Steele, I'm Inspector Gomez."

He waved me to a chair and sat down himself, smoothing out a sheet of paper which he leaned forward to read.

Scary thoughts had run through my head as we approached the police station. Horrifying stories had leaked about Cuban jails such as Presidio Modelo, the huge circular prison on Isla de la Juventud. That facility was closed in 1967 after many reports of torture, both before Fidel and after.

I felt in my pocket for Bruno's phone which I feared might soon be taken from me. I was glad I had spoken to Mimi earlier.

I waited for fifteen minutes in a windowless room alone with my thoughts before the door opened and in came Gomez, the instrument of my fate, a physically unimpressive middle-aged man, short and balding in police uniform. I stood up for some reason, it seemed polite.

"You are British?"

"That's right."

"But you came here from Toronto?"

"I did, yes."

"What brings you here?"

"It's a beautiful country."

"Where are you staying?"

"I'm touring around."

"Where did you stay last night?"

"At a guest house in the town."

"Its name?"

"Magnolia."

He pushed the page away, leaned back in his chair and frowned.

"We have a seriously injured man."

"I know, I reported it. He is my friend."

He sighed.

"A tourist, eh? Tourism is important to the Cuban economy. But so is law and order. Why shouldn't I arrest you for assault?"

"You would be arresting the wrong person. I have done nothing. I simply went to stroll round the square and when I returned I was shocked to find my friend unconscious. I was certainly not responsible for the attack."

"Then who was?"

The absurdity of the situation then hit me. Should I tell the Inspector the truth? That Bruno's attacker was the chief of police of the province? This man's boss! Not a good idea. Anyway, don't lie if you can avoid it, I told myself, that's never prudent.

In the end all I could manage was a silent shrug.

The officer sighed and stood up.

"We are going to have to hold you here for the time being," he said flatly.

I almost felt sympathy for him. He was doing his job as he saw it. In his shoes I might have behaved the same way.

"I'd like to speak to a lawyer," I said.

He smiled sourly. "I see you watch the movies."

"What's that supposed to mean?"

"Cubans respect stability and order. But our process is not like yours. In Britain or the United States there would be public defenders eager to come and represent you. Here, things are different."

"Can I make a phone call, at least?"

He nodded. "I don't see why not. I see you have a phone. We shall have to take that away but you may make a call first."

"Thank you. I should like privacy."

He nodded. "That's reasonable." He left the room.

. . .

Kathy heard the phone ring in her suite at the Residencia Magnifica on Cayo Santa Maria.

"Yes?"

"It's Oliver."

"Where are you?"

"In jail."

He explained.

"Oh brilliant," she said.

"Thanks. Any ideas about getting me out of here?"

"Let me work on it. I'll be there in the morning."

"I trust you."

"Count on it. I hope you had a chance to eat earlier, by the way. They say prison food is disgusting."

"Oh, go and enjoy grilled prawns and a nice steak at your damn hotel."

"I think I shall. See you tomorrow."

But when she made some phone calls to Havana shortly afterwards, the banter gave way to deadly earnest.

I spent a wretched night in an airless cell with a bench and a bug-ridden straw mat that I shared with a family of cockroaches.

The roaches took the position that I was the one trespassing. I got no sleep and was bleary eyed when they fetched me next morning and led me, unshaven, to the interview room.

In walked Kathy and winked at me. With her was a well-groomed man in a neat grey suit with a permanent smile. He was portly and looked well fed and quietly pleased with himself.

"This is Nelson de Silva Ruz, senior partner in the Havana law firm of de Silva Ruz and Perez."

I saw Inspector Gomez blink as Ruz was introduced, but I didn't understand why.

Twenty minutes of polite but forceful discussion between Ruz and Gomez. I was surprised by the deference the policeman showed the lawyer.

Finally, Ruz turned to me and said, "Here's what has been agreed. You will be released. Your belongings will be returned. That's the good news."

I felt overwhelming relief. Anything was better than going back to that wretched cell.

But whatever bad news Ruz could give me must be pretty awful to outweigh the good.

He saw my relief and smiled gravely. "I'm afraid you must remain in Cuba for now. The police are keeping your passport, pending investigation."

"What sort of investigation?"

"They are concerned by the vicious attack on your friend Bruno. When he recovers and can confirm what happened, no doubt your innocence will be evident and all will be well." He caught my eye and held it for a second. He obviously had more to say but not in front of Gomez.

I nodded. "Of course." I turned to Gomez. I felt like saying, 'Your accommodations suck.' What I actually said was, "Thank you for your understanding. Naturally I shall be at your disposal to resolve everything as soon as possible."

He nodded curtly. He did not look happy but I really didn't care and five minutes later I was free.

"We can talk in my car," said Ruz. He had a large black Mercedes. He turned on the engine which was almost silent, and ran the air conditioning. The interior was furnished in a pale honey-coloured fabric and I sat gingerly in the back seat, anxious not to transfer prison grime from my grubby clothing.

"I'm really grateful. I've no idea what you said to Gomez but it seemed to do the trick."

The attorney smiled. "He was, let's say, ready to be persuaded."

Kathy explained. "Nelson is a fine lawyer, of course. But he is also fortunate to have an interesting last name."

"What's that?"

"Ruz."

"I don't understand."

"Fidel Castro's full name is Fidel Castro Ruz. Ruz was his mother's name."

I stared at the dapper attorney. "You are related to Fidel?"

"A distant cousin," said Kathy.

Ruz smiled broadly. "So distant, in fact, that Fidel may not know of the connection."

"It hasn't hurt your career, though," prompted Kathy.

"My friends in the legal community know the link is remote. But I must say, when dealing with mid-level officialdom it's very helpful."

We waved Ruz goodbye and he headed back to Havana, after giving us his card and assuring us that if anything else came up he would jump on it.

"A good man," I said.

"Sure is."

"Where did you find him?"

"He was recommended."

"By whom?"

"His firm does some work for a company of Carlton Tisch's in England that imports cigars. He is really a corporate-type lawyer who specializes in insurance and shipping, stuff like that."

"Seems to be able to handle anything, though."

"Sure does."

A thought struck me. "I wonder how he gets paid?"

"I was curious about that," said Kathy. "I asked Mimi and Mimi asked Carlton. Carlton said don't ask too many questions."

"How do you spell 'hard currency?'"

"Exactly."

Kathy had a rental car. We drove to the hospital to see Bruno. He looked weak but he was sitting up in bed and beamed when we walked in. I suspected the police would be in to question him soon, so I explained the cover story Ruz had worked out and coached him in his responses.

"We'll see you in a day or two," I said.

He looked anxious. "Where are you going?"

"We're not deserting you, don't worry. But I could use some R and R so we're going back to Kathy's hotel which is a plush new gin palace on Cayo Santa Maria."

"I've heard those places are pretty comfortable," he said wistfully.

I said, "We need to figure out what's going on with Rothman, Cruz and whoever else is involved in this witches' brew. For that we need somewhere with good communications."

"Oh sure. Go!"

54

In Havana, Martin had a lecture scheduled at the University. He saw no reason not to return to his normal routine so he left home and headed for the campus as if nothing had happened. He stopped on the way as usual, to have his shoes polished.

Caleb acknowledged him with a subdued nod.

"A fine morning," observed Martin, sitting in the raised chair in the shadow of a fig tree.

The old man shrugged and dabbed some cheap polish on Martin's shoes.

"Problems?" Martin asked.

"You could say so." And the whole sad story about the cancelled concert came out. Caleb's disappointment was plain to see.

Martin listened sympathetically. "Why do you think the backer dropped out?"

Caleb shrugged. "Beats me. It doesn't really matter. Some big corporation by the sound of it. There are so many in the *Estados Unidos*. They have their ways of doing business, right or wrong. If they didn't see a future for the group, I guess it was their right to cancel their investment."

"Who do you think it was?"

"The backer? I never heard the name. Pepe said they owned casinos. He mentioned one – Portabella or something like that." Caleb laughed. "Made me think of mushrooms."

"Portofino, perhaps?"

"That's it. Portofino. May they fail miserably, though I'm sure they won't. Those *Yanquis* know how to make money."

Martin wondered if there was a connection between the abrupt closing of Café Hola and Stanley Rothman's issues with Hector Cruz. Portofino was a large corporation and it was possible that one hand did not know what the other was doing. But it might also be that Rothman was cleaning up his act. He had sailed very close to the wind in subsidising Cruz and he may have decided to get right with the authorities by cutting out an illegal investment that the Cubans could fault him for.

From Caleb's point of view, as the old singer said, it didn't make much difference. He was out of a job and back shining shoes.

"Never mind, old friend. Tomorrow is another day." Martin pressed a few extra coins into the elderly man's palm. He was aware that they were no real consolation but he was at a loss for a more meaningful gesture.

But as he walked, his mind was turning over. He was well connected in musical circles within the University, through his piano playing and his love of jazz. Havana was a small town in some ways and he had connections, people he could mention Caleb to. He could make introductions at least. After that it would be up to the old man to show if he had what it took.

55

STANLEY ROTHMAN FINISHED READING the Cruz file and looked up at Mimi. "I didn't realise what a small timer this guy is. If I'd known, I'd have offered him less money."

"Money?"

He frowned. "Forget I said that. Just rambling."

But things were starting to make sense to Mimi. A smile spread over her face and she relaxed visibly. She looked round the room and, seeing a comfortable sofa, strolled over and sat down.

"Nice to take the weight off my feet."

He frowned, clearly not expecting that.

She laughed. "Relax Stanley. Loosen up. Have your stooge fix us a drink and we can thrash this out."

He frowned. "You're being very personal."

"Oh, we've met."

"Where?"

"At a couple of dinners. And you spoke at an investors conference in Las Vegas several years ago. My husband – he was just my fiancé in those days – was on the panel, in fact you came to his cocktail party."

His eyes narrowed. "Who are you?"

She grinned. "Mimi."

"I know that from your passport. Mimi Entwistle."

"I'm only using that name because it's on my British passport, which is as old as heck. I didn't want to confuse the Cuban authorities. My married name is Tisch."

There was a long pause. Rothman was rearranging some facts in his mind. He didn't seem to like the result. "You are Carlton Tisch's wife?"

"Exactly."

"Well damn. What the heck are you doing in Havana?"

"I might ask you the same question. Where are those drinks, by the way?"

Irritated, Rothman gestured to his man. "Fetch us something."

Mimi waited until he was out of the room and then slipped a hand in her purse, felt for her phone and pressed the speed dial key for Kathy.

Rothman did not see the phone because it was hidden in her purse. He heard a dial tone but did not realise she was making a call until it was answered and she withdrew the phone and put it to her ear.

"Kathy? Guess who I'm with!"

Rothman saw what she was up to and tried to snatch the phone away but she was too quick. She leaped up, putting the sofa between them, and went on speaking. "Stanley Rothman. Yes, Rothman the casino guy. He just had me kidnapped and has taken away the Cruz file."

At the mention of his name, Rothman stopped chasing her. His face went red. He stood fuming as he realised he had been tricked.

Mimi was still talking. "I'll fill you in later. Bottom line, I don't think he's a very nice person."

She rang off and smiled at Rothman without warmth. "So here we are, Stanley, and if I may say so I think you're in a bind."

"What do you mean?"

"Well let's see. You are a casino operator. You are in Havana. And you've been talking to a senior police officer with political ambitions."

"So what?"

"Must I spell it out? There's only one explanation that accounts for all that. You plan to get into the casino business."

He frowned. "I'm not breaking any laws."

"No American laws. Although there may be a spot of bribery going on that would trip you up under the Foreign Corrupt Practices Act. But I doubt if the Castros would stand for such a gross betrayal of the revolution."

He shook his head. "No money has changed hands."

She ignored the remark. "What will happen when the Castros hear about you and Cruz? An American investor collaborating with a serving police officer to open a casino? Sounds like a capital offence to me. "

"You are exaggerating."

"Am I? A lot of people flew too close to the sun and got their wings clipped by the Castros. This island would get too hot for you in a hurry."

He tried a different tack and forced a smile. "I understand what Tisch saw in you. Not just a pretty face." But he knew she was right. He walked over to the window and looked out. The sun was setting over the Florida Straits. Lost in the haze were Key West and the United States, a country of laws. But here the law was the Castros. He turned to Mimi with a scowl.

"I can stop you from leaving here."

"A few minutes ago, maybe. But I saw your face when I made that phone call. The cat's out of the bag."

"Who were you talking to?"

"Someone called Kathy Smith. She works with my husband."

"Where is she?"

"Somewhere in Cuba. She is now calling Carlton who will hear that you kidnapped me and brought me to a house in Havana against my will. And Carlton is not a forgiving person, trust me."

Another long pause.

"What do you want?" he gritted.

"For myself, not much. But there are some decent Cubans whose safety depends on my keeping hold of that dossier. I want it back."

He gestured towards the table where the file lay and she strolled over and picked it up.

The man appeared with a tray with two tall glasses containing a concoction of colourless liquid and various macerated greenery. She raised a glass to Rothman and took a long sip.

"Delicious. Now I'd like a ride back to my hotel."

56

"SORRY, MY FRIEND," Hector Cruz muttered.

He had finally worn through the yellow plastic ties, exulting as he felt them come apart but forcing himself not to indicate to Bruno by any motion that he was free. Slowly he adjusted his posture in the back of the van.

Bruno had been thinking of lighting a cigarette but refrained out of consideration for his prisoner. Cruz repaid the courtesy by reaching forward, putting his hands round Bruno's neck and slamming his head against the door pillar.

The impact was violent, denting the metal pillar. Bruno slumped in his seat unconscious.

Cruz rifled Bruno's pockets looking for money and extracted a wad of small bills from the young man's hip pocket.

He climbed out of the van and marched away and around the corner as fast as possible, slowing only when he was out of sight of the vehicle. He looked around for a payphone and called his Santa Clara regional headquarters which was separate from the regular PNR police station.

Minutes later he was sitting in a quiet office with a phone at his disposal and attentive subordinates bringing him iced water.

He took stock. It was not a pleasant process. Too much had gone wrong. In the last twenty-four hours the American, Feaver, had been snatched from his grasp on Cayo Piedra. He had also been forced to release the hated intellectual Sanchez Madera and his wife. Worse still, he had no idea where the incriminating file was. He hoped it was in the hands of Stanley Rothman rather than with Steele's American woman friend. At least Rothman wouldn't hand it over to the Cuban Ministry of the Interior, since it contained references that would embarrass Rothman himself.

But it also put Cruz at Rothman's mercy and that worried him. He didn't trust the devious old casino owner any further than he could flip a fifty dollar chip. He phoned Rothman's cellphone number.

"Yes?"

"It's Hector Cruz."

"Oh, it's you. What do you want?"

Cruz related the dismal series of events. When he was finished there was silence on the line.

"Are you there?" asked Cruz.

"Yes. What do you need from me?"

To say Rothman's tone was cold would be an understatement.

"I just wanted to fill you in. I'm taking steps to rectify the situation." It was the best he could think to say. After the call ended he stood up and kicked the desk in fury. The wood splintered and a secretary came running. He waved her away.

His brain was in turmoil but one thought was uppermost. He wanted satisfaction. Wherever the file was, he would find it but meanwhile he would start by finding Oliver Steele and getting his revenge.

Steele couldn't have gone far, he reasoned. He started by sending a police car round to the street where Bruno's van had been parked, but the van was no longer there so he assumed Oliver had driven it away. He ordered an alert throughout the province of Villa Clara for an Englishman in a white van. Having done that, he checked into a hotel in Santa Clara, showered and went to bed in a foul mood.

Around noon there was a call from the local PNR office. It was Inspector Gomez.

"We received your alert about the Englishman."

"Yes?"

"Too late, I'm afraid. We arrested him yesterday and held him overnight but today he was released."

The inspector must have realised he brought unwelcome news because he tried to mollify Cruz. "We have his passport so he can't leave the country."

"Where was he headed?"

"He was with an American woman who is staying at the Residencia Magnifica on Cayo Santa Maria."

57

"MORE POLICE? WHAT DO THEY WANT?" I asked.

I was dozing in the passenger seat of Kathy's car when we jolted to a halt. A uniformed guard, rifle at the ready, approached the car.

I looked round. We were at some kind of checkpoint.

"Don't worry, I'm prepared." She wound down the window and handed the guard a sheet of paper which he scanned suspiciously. Apparently it passed muster because he waved us on.

I looked at the note. "This is just an email confirming your hotel reservation."

"It's enough. You are now entering a different Cuba. This is the region designed for high-end tourists."

"Why the checkpoint?"

"I guess they don't want any old riff raff lowering the tone."

We drove out on a narrow sandy key barely wider than the road itself. It stretched into the distance. It reminded me of remoter stretches of the Florida Keys with sea all around and blue sky above.

We drove for fifteen miles with nothing to see before the causeway widened and curved round. We turned off the road and passed through monumental stone gates. There was a long driveway and then we swished to a halt in the forecourt of a huge modern hotel.

"You don't have a passport so it's going to be difficult to check you in," said Kathy. "We'll sneak you straight up to the room. We'll bribe the maid if she notices anything."

"I have dollars," I said.

"That will help. You can change them into CUCs at reception. And you can use your British credit card."

"Money talks, even in Cuba?"

"Especially in Cuba."

"What I really need is a shower," I said.

She hailed an electric golf cart. "Jump aboard."

She gave the driver her room number and the cart swished away down a paved pathway surrounded by lush, well-watered bushes. The rooms were in a series of two-storey houses set among the gardens. I looked around. "Nice and secluded."

I washed the jailhouse grime from my body under a hot shower. I was starting to feel better about the whole business. Kon was free. So were Martin and Sylvia Sanchez Madera. Bruno was recovering from his concussion and the dreaded Hector Cruz had apparently been neutralised.

True, I was required to stay in Cuba but it should only be for a few days. And I was surrounded by creature comforts in a luxury hotel. Things could be worse.

Kathy threw a bottle of suntan oil and the latest Carl Hiaasen novel in a beach bag and announced she was going for a swim. I felt sufficiently relaxed to stroll back to the front desk and enquire if the hotel had a squash court.

I was told by the bell captain, regrettably no. But as he was speaking, someone tapped me on the shoulder. I turned to see an individual of medium height and athletic build.

"Not much squash in Cuba I'm afraid." His accent was British with a faint hint of the United States somewhere in the background.

"So I'm hearing. I'm Oliver Steele. I don't think we've met."

"Clark. Sandy Clark. There's something else that might appeal to you, though. Have you heard of frontenis?"

I admitted I had not.

"What about jai alai?"

"Of course." I had watched the high speed Basque court game played in the Pyrenees and also, in a debased commercial form, in Florida.

"Imagine jai alai played with a tennis racquet and a rubber ball and you have frontenis."

"And is it played here?"

The bell captain was listening and interjected. "Widely. There is a fronton in Remedios. Would you like me to see if I can make a reservation?"

We looked at each other. "Why not?"

The bell captain made a phone call. "There is an opening at three o'clock today."

I looked at Sandy Clark. "What do you think? Lunch first?"

"Perfect."

I learned that he was a California physician, in Cuba for a medical conference. We ordered sandwiches on the terrace. *Mojitos* flowed although, not knowing my opponent's skill level and always preferring to win, I confined myself to one.

After lunch we took a taxi into Remedios. Gaspar, the club professional, greeted us.

"Glad to see interest in our sport," he said. "Come on back, there's a doubles match in progress."

A fronton is basically a very long room with one of its sides missing. Spectators can watch the players hitting a ball up and down the length of the court.

Four young Cubans were hammering the ball with great force. It flew to the front wall like a bullet, rebounding so fast I could hardly see it. I had to admire their athleticism as they smote the ball with powerful squash-type strokes.

The players finished and left the court. "Want to try?" asked Gaspar.

"Why not?

He handed me a racquet. The ball looked similar to that used in racquetball.

I am used to squash, where it is generally better to hit the ball along the side wall. In frontenis, by contrast, it can pay to steer the ball to the centre of the court, forcing your opponent to move his feet to one side or the other to get a good swing.

Dr. Clark seemed to have grasped this principle because he strolled on court and unleashed a stream of powerful forehand and backhand drives to win the game. When I complimented him he gave me a pitying look. "What you failed to understand, young man, is the *Mojito* factor. The more *Mojitos* you consume, the better your play. At lunch you only had one *Mojito*. I had two. The result: defeat for you, victory for me."

"A novel theory."

He shrugged. "It's a scientific fact."

I spoke to Gaspar afterwards. "I'm curious. The average Cuban earns $25 a month. A racquet must cost at least that, a month's wages."

He nodded. "It's true. Another major expense is footwear. The floors of the courts, many of them outdoors, are hard on shoes."

"So how can anyone afford to play the game?"

He laughed. "Now there's a metaphor for life in Cuba," he said. "It is impossible, and yet it happens."

Apparently frontenis was for athletes with access to tourist dollars and people like our Havana lawyer who did business with foreigners.

That evening, Kathy surprised me by producing a black lace cocktail dress and wriggling into it. It looked expensive. She saw my surprise.

"Zip me up," she grinned.

I obliged. "I didn't know you travelled with this kind of kit."

"I clean up well when I want to. Besides, we're celebrating."

58

BEHIND A JUNIPER BUSH in the immaculate grounds of the Residencia Magnifica, Hector Cruz checked his silenced Beretta. He had a full clip.

There had been no problem driving to the hotel. He was in plain clothes, driving an unmarked car, but when he identified himself to the police at the Cayo Santa Maria checkpoint they waved him through with fawning respect.

The hotel desk staff had readily given him Kathy's room number. He declined their offer to accompany him there.

Things were in a different mode now, Cruz told himself. One on one, *mano a mano*. The violent side of his nature, always present, had grown to critical level. The general who had warned Raul Castro against giving Cruz too much power was prescient. The policeman was out of control.

Not that this was apparent to Cruz himself. He felt as cool as a chilled *Mojito* and completely rational as he lay in wait for Oliver and Kathy to return from dinner.

He heard their footfall and murmurs of conversation as they approached. He shifted position so as to have an unobstructed view of the door to Kathy's room and prepared to take aim.

AFTER DINNER, Kathy and I strolled back to the room arm in arm. Our building was at the far edge of the estate, some way from the dining room.

It was dark and we missed the path a couple of times. We finally got it right and reached our doorway laughing and mellow. Kathy took her magnetic card from her purse and waved it at the lock.

The soft thump of a silenced gunshot came from the shrubbery nearby and I sensed the breeze as a bullet embedded itself in the wood of the door, inches from Kathy's arm. I pulled her roughly away from the lighted door and into darkness.

I had nothing to use as a weapon.

"GET INSIDE," I shouted. I pushed the door open and gave her a helping shove.

"Stay there." I slammed the door shut behind her.

Another shot slammed into the wall. I leaped aside into protective darkness.

Beyond the short radius of light thrown by the lamp on the building, the next light source was a street lamp a hundred feet away. Between the two, all was dark with hardly outlines visible.

Somewhere in that dark pool was my assailant. Would he retreat or try again and, if so, from what angle?

I tiptoed towards a place in the darkness midway between the two light sources and paused to get used to the darkness, keeping absolutely still and listening hard.

It was at least a minute before I heard a rustle, surprisingly close. I waited and heard it again. It came from less than four feet away. Armed attacker, unarmed defender – me. Bad odds. Options? Not many and none good.

I launched myself forward in a rugby tackle.

In American football, a player will often hurl himself at his opponent, using body weight to stop him. In rugby, where players are less densely packed on the field and usually moving at a run, you launch yourself on a much lower trajectory, around knee height. A clean hit will unbalance and topple your opponent. That took me back a few years to my time at boarding school but it was worth a try – by attacking low down I was less likely to be hit by a bullet.

I hit someone's shins, low and sideways-on. In the tangle of thrashing limbs, I tried desperately to find my target's gun arm. Surprised, he strained furiously. I couldn't speak to his fitness but he sure as heck felt stronger and heavier than me.

As we wrestled on the ground I slid an arm round his neck and for the first time got a feeling for where our bodies were, relative to one other. I groped for his right shoulder and forced my hand towards his wrist, feeling for a gun. Lord, please make him not left-handed.

You sometimes read reports of murder trials

where the accused, coached by his attorney, switches to the impersonal voice. *Shots were fired. A situation was encountered.* Or the ever-popular *'everything went black.'* I've been cynical about those accounts in the past but, having now seen things first hand, I know what they mean. Because shots *were* fired. Not by me, by the other guy. My hand was over his and the bullets, or one of them, went into his body. He ceased to struggle and went limp.

I had Bruno's cell phone in my pocket. I fished it out and shone its dim light on my opponent.

I was not really surprised to see that Hector Cruz had been shot dead.

I lay motionless for several minutes, recovering my breath and wondering what to do next. I had contributed to the death of a senior Cuban police officer. Safe to say that any defence I might try to offer along the lines of 'he attacked me first' wouldn't carry much weight in these parts.

Apparently he was alone, certainly there was no sign of supporters. Did his colleagues know where he was? If not, that might be my saving grace. By the light of my phone screen I established that we were in a maintenance area. There was a large mound of logs and branches piled against a shed and I dragged Cruz's body across and basically buried it underneath them. There was no knowing when it would be discovered but at least it was out of sight for now.

I returned to the bedroom and tapped on the door.

"It's me. The coast is clear."

She let me in, then replaced the deadbolt and chain securing the door. "You look a mess. What happened?"

"There was a struggle, then he ran away," I lied. "I don't think he'll be back tonight." That at least was true.

She looked far from happy about the situation, so I made a show of locking the big plate glass window. I took the side of the bed nearer the window and put my pistol, loaded and ready, on the nightstand.

61

IN THE DAWN light I brewed two cups of hotel coffee and carried them back to the bed.

"I've had enough of this," I said. "I'm leaving."

"Are you sure?"

"Damn right I'm sure. You should come too, it's not safe here. Book us a flight to Florida this afternoon."

She shook her head. "You can't do that. I can, but you can't."

"Why not?"

"A couple of reasons. For starters, you arrived from Toronto. You can't just jump on a plane to the United States."

"What else?"

"You don't have your British passport. The police

kept it. Even if you tried to return via Canada, Cuba wouldn't let you. You aren't legal."

"I have my U.S. passport."

"Wouldn't work. They match exits with entries and as a U.S. citizen technically you never arrived. You can't leave Cuba!"

"There must be a way. Can't we bribe someone?"

She shook her head. "I wouldn't care to try it."

So I was marooned in Cuba. But I really don't like being told what I can and can't do. I decided to go and talk to Bruno – Bruno the fixer.

I borrowed the car from Kathy while she was getting a massage at the hotel spa. When I say 'borrowed,' I didn't actually ask her permission because I knew I would get an argument about insurance, my name not being on the lease and so on. But the truth is I was angry. Being shot at, even in the grounds of a nice hotel, can have that effect. And when I'm upset I tend to barrel ahead where cooler heads might stop and think.

I drove to the hospital. Bruno was still in bed but looking stronger. He said they were releasing him that day. We talked and the name of our friend Sinbad came up.

Later I picked up Kathy at the hotel and said, "Let's go for a drive, I want to show you something."

We drove back to the mainland, to Caibarién. It was the first time I had been there in daylight. It had once been one of the busiest ports in Cuba according to the guidebook but in the sun I could see many of the remaining colonial houses were collapsing through disuse and neglect. There was a depressed air about the place.

We drove through town and stopped a mile outside. I parked the car at a fishing quay near a ramshackle shed and we went inside.

The first person we met was Sinbad.

When you've been through danger with some-one, even if you've only known them for a day or so, it can form a powerful bond. I couldn't help myself, I went up and hugged him before stepping back and introducing Kathy.

"This salt-caked sailor saved our lives – with a vengeance."

She laughed and they shook hands.

"I'm glad to see you," I said. "Until I spoke to Bruno I assumed you were on the high seas, plying your trade between Pinar del Rio and Cancun."

He nodded. "I let José handle the trip to Cancun. He's been wanting to do one on his own and he's a good seaman; my presence wasn't essential."

I noticed that without Bruno there to translate he spoke English pretty well.

"Talking of good seamen, I may need your services again," I said.

"Bruno told me."

Kathy looked at me. "What do you mean?"

"I'm tired of being shot at. I'm going back to Florida by boat."

Sinbad nodded. "The vessel should be back from Pinar in a couple of hours. We can leave tonight if it's urgent."

"That's what I'd like."

"Rather you than me," said Kathy. "Ten hours bobbing around in a tiny boat in the shark-infested Florida Straits, dodging Coastguards and getting sick? I have a reservation on a nice flight home with my tour group next week. That suits me fine."

"I understand," I said. "But I need to do it."

"What about your passport?" she asked.

"The police can keep it as a souvenir. I still have my U.S. one. I just shan't be able to come back to Cuba, at least not until the regime changes."

"So, no more British passport?"

"I'll tell the Brits I lost it, which is sort of true. I can probably get it replaced."

She sighed. "If you're sure."

"I am."

"Do you need to go back to the hotel?"

"No. I don't want to risk being seen again. I'll hang out here for a few hours, until we leave."

"Okay," she said. Her tone said, 'I think you're crazy but it's your neck.'

"Well that's settled," said Sinbad.

"I think I'll head back to the hotel," said Kathy looking at her watch. "Might be in time for the lunch buffet. I fancy garlic chicken with black beans and fried bananas, then an afternoon with a novel on the beach."

"Knock yourself out," I said.

"I'll just check in with our tour leader." She took out her phone and dialled. "Hi Brittany, how's it going? Today's a free day, right?"

As she listened, her face went still.

"When?" she asked. "Did they say why?" Then, "Are they still there?"

She rang off and looked at us. "The police are at the hotel, armed and looking to make an arrest. Brittany says they are hostile. She's pretty upset."

I shrugged. 'Well that confirms my decision. I stay right here until we leave."

She stared at me, white faced. "They weren't looking for you. They were looking for me!"

We let that sink in. Finally, Sinbad opened a drawer and took out a small packet which he handed to Kathy.

"What's this?" she said.

"Seasick pills."

. . .

In the last few days, Hurricane Matthew had been lurking offshore. On October 5th it roared through Haiti, claiming 900 lives. Then it hit Cuba, devastating the small town of Baracoa on the island's north-eastern tip.

Giant waves destroyed cement buildings. 75 mile an hour winds reduced much of the town to rubble. From there it proceeded west in the general direction of Havana and Caibarién where Oliver and his friends were, so time was of the essence.

62

"WE NEED to do something about Kathy's car," said Sinbad.

I knew what he meant. The car was sitting in the street outside and although there was nothing illegal about that, its plates identified it as a rented vehicle, not something a fisherman would use. Sinbad had not said anything about the risk he was running by helping us out but I had not overlooked it.

Kathy looked scared, frankly. Fear was not an emotion I associated with her and I put it down to surprise. I myself had been afraid almost constantly since arriving in Cuba – the dual nature of the sunny but repressive island weighed on me like a lead shroud – but the fear had become familiar and I had built a protective shell against it.

Kathy, on the other hand, had spent her time in a

smart hotel far from physical danger, at least until last night's assassination attempt.

"We'll get through this," I said.

She tried to smile. "Sure we will."

"You have the right stuff," I said, meaning it.

"So, my friends. The car?" said Sinbad.

I said. "We should move it as far away from your premises as possible."

"My thought too."

"Shall we drive it to Remedios and leave it in the centre of town? Then it would give no clue as to where Kathy went."

Sinbad nodded agreement.

"Let's do it," said Kathy.

"It's better if I drive," I said. "You are high profile at present, young white woman a in rented car, wanted by the police."

She half smiled. "Okay. Buy me a toothbrush while you're about it."

Sinbad and I went outside. The Toyota was smart and shiny, rental plates prominent. I looked at him. "Too clean?"

He nodded.

We hosed the vehicle down in order to wet its surface and then scattered mud and dust on it. When we were done it had aged ten years. Sinbad unscrewed the tell-tale plates and tossed them in the boot. Now we had an anonymous car.

He grinned. "That looks better – more Cuban."

We drove into Remedios. Sinbad drove his truck and I followed in the Toyota. Near the centre of town he pulled into a quiet street and told me to park by the kerb. I left the keys under the seat. Then I climbed into Sinbad's truck and we drove off.

On the way back we stopped at a store where I picked out a toothbrush for Kathy and Sinbad bought bread and cheese and some chocolate.

"For the trip," he said.

I produced some Convertible pesos and offered to pay but he waved them away, paying with Cuban pesos.

Once in the truck he explained, "They would have taken your money and changed it later but there was no point in appearing 'foreign.' It would leave a trail."

Back at Sinbad's it was growing dark.

"Can't we start?" I asked.

Sinbad shook his head.

"We could sail out there, not looking as if we were crossing, just putting ourselves in position, getting a bit closer. It would save some time," I said.

"But we have to watch out for Coastguard."

"How can they tell if someone is trying to cross to Florida?"

"They use their judgment. It is usually obvious because the boat is loaded with guilty-looking people. Our case is different but, if in doubt, they will turn you back."

"How bad would that be?"

"Quite bad. The penalty for a first time offender can be fairly mild, as little as a warning and a fine. But you and Kathy aren't regular Cubans, you are foreigners wanted by the police. As the English say, your goose would be cooked."

"Yours too, for helping us?"

He nodded. "Since you mention it."

So we waited another two hours before leaving. Finally, we set out.

"Nice and dark now," I remarked, but Sinbad shook his head. "There is a new moon; it will rise later."

"Will the sea be calm?" asked Kathy. She was pleased with the toothbrush but was still worried about seasickness.

"The forecast is mixed," said Sinbad. "The hurricane is still some way east of us but it has moved past Haiti. Now it is threatening the north-east tip of Cuba several hundred miles from here. We may still run into rain and high winds in the middle of the Straits."

"Does that mean big waves? Won't a small boat like this capsize?" asked Kathy. I wouldn't say she was panicking but her voice rose noticeably.

Sinbad looked at her. His craggy, weather-beaten face smiled in a way I knew was meant to be encouraging. "You are right, Madame. This is a small boat. Things will be uncomfortable. But I have sailed these seas for forty years, often in conditions as bad as we may meet tonight, and as you see I am still alive."

From our brief acquaintance I knew Sinbad to be honest rather than diplomatic so I personally felt reassured but, as he said, there was real risk. We were in for a rough ride.

"He knows what he's doing," I said. "I can vouch for that."

"I sure hope so."

"We'll be fine." I tried not to sound impatient. I wished she would leave the subject alone. It was not as if we had a choice.

We pulled away from shore, Kathy staring back nervously at the few lights of Caibarién as they faded into the distance.

Soon we were alone in the darkness. There was only a moderate swell but it was greater than we had experienced on the way to Cayo Piedra. Sinbad was steering with one hand on the wheel, humming to himself and glancing now and then at the compass which was illuminated by a faint blue light.

"I'm hungry," I said. "What about fixing something to eat?" I really wanted to give Kathy something to think about. She took a loaf out of the bag we had brought and tore it into pieces, then sliced some cheese and made sandwiches which she handed round.

While she was at the other end of the boat, Sinbad took me aside. "I didn't want to scare her," he said, "but the weather is going to be bad. The hurricane is still some way away but it is moving towards us and there will be feeder bands."

"Big waves?"

"Bigger than this little craft."

"So we'll need to hold on tight?"

"You've got the picture."

We cruised peacefully for an hour, out of sight of land. As Sinbad predicted, the new moon was a little fuller than when we sailed to Cayo Piedra; it shone through intermittent cloud. At times the sea's surface gleamed appealingly, but moments later all would be black as pitch.

In one of the dark intervals he tapped my shoulder and pointed ahead. I saw a pinpoint of light.

"What is it?"

"Probably Coastguard."

"What should we do?"

"First, we make a U-turn before they spot us and figure out which way we were heading. Then we pretend. Remember, this is a fishing boat." He indicated the heaped nets in the stern and the fish slopping in the tank made for that purpose, fish he and I had diligently tossed in there a few hours before. "We are fishermen and you are my assistant."

"What about Kathy?"

"We need to get her out of sight."

We called her back and explained the situation. She gave me an 'I told you so' look but consented to being laid on the floor of the vessel and covered with a greasy tarpaulin that smelled heavily of fish.

"What if they ask me questions?" I asked Sinbad.

He looked grim. "Pray that they don't."

As the Coastguard drew alongside, a powerful spotlight shone in our faces and there was a shouted command. Sinbad waved acknowledgment and slowed to a halt, putting the engine in neutral.

The Coastguard vessel was over a hundred feet long and much higher in the water than us. An officer leaned over the side and fired a series of questions at Sinbad, whose rumbling answers, I could tell, communicated respect. I caught the words 'Caibarién' and 'pescador' as he indicated the pile of nets and our meagre catch heaped in the chest.

The officer turned to look at me and barked a question in Spanish. I had no idea what it meant. I nodded and shrugged, hoping it looked like a Cuban shrug.

"He's a little touched, he doesn't speak," explained Sinbad.

The officer gave me a long stare, then turned away. He fired a couple more sentences at Sinbad, pointing to the sky as he did so, and then disappeared. Sinbad increased engine speed and we headed back towards Cuba.

A quarter of an hour later the Coastguard boat was out of sight.

"Have they gone?" I asked.

"Probably. We'll give them a few more minutes, just to be on the safe side."

Finally, he turned the boat in a wide arc.

"So have we lost half an hour cruising in the wrong direction?" I asked.

He nodded. "Yes. But it's better than being carted off to jail."

"What did the officer say?" I asked.

"He wanted to know why we were out so late. I told him we had been fishing off Matanzas and were on our way home to Caibarién. We were a bit off course but he seemed to buy it." He laughed. "I don't think he has a high opinion of my navigation."

"What if we meet them again?"

Sinbad shook his head. "We won't. They are in a hurry to get home because of the storm." He hesitated. "He advised us to do the same."

There was movement on the floor. "Can I come out now?" Kathy shook herself free of the tarpaulins. "God that canvas stinks."

"How are we doing?" I asked Sinbad, three hours later. By my reckoning we were about half way.

"We're making average time."

63

WHEN THE STORM CAME, it came suddenly.

"Hold onto something," Sinbad yelled over his shoulder.

I needed no encouragement.

The first drops of warm rain fell softly but within seconds they became a violent deluge. Sinbad donned a lifejacket and made Kathy and me do the same. I had barely strapped it on when the wind arrived, great gusts that whipped the waves around us into huge fractured dunes. The little boat slid down the side of one before lurching up the other, only to rocket past the crest and swoop into the next trough.

Sinbad wrestled the wheel, trying desperately to keep the bow heading into the waves.

Kathy was having a problem. Soaking wet, with

less physical strength, she was being tossed violently from side to side. Fair haired Kathy had given way to drenched Kathy, her blonde mane flattened to a dark skullcap, her nipples prominent under the sodden tee shirt. Her face was set in a half smile as if to say 'I'm damned if I'll let a little weather get the better of me.'

I found a length of rope in the bilges and stumbled over to her. I fastened one end tight around her waist and tied the other to a cleat on the rail so that if she fell overboard at least she would still be attached.

The wind and rain lashed us for several minutes then ceased as suddenly as they had come. An eerie calm followed.

"That was intense," said Kathy, her voice shaking.

Sinbad said nothing, his face grim. I read his expression.

"It will come back, won't it?"

He nodded. "Worse."

Five minutes later it started again. The boat seemed to stand vertically on its end and several times I was sure we were finished. In the maelstrom the fish tank went flying, along with its contents and anything else that was not tied down and Kathy had reason to bless the crude lifeline I had cobbled together. Things died down briefly, then blew up again. The pattern was repeated again and again for about an hour.

Finally there was an extended calm. Sinbad turned to me and said, "I think that's it. There's a silver lining. The wind has been blowing us in the direction we want to go. We've probably saved half an hour of travelling time."

"Is the storm over?" Kathy asked.

"Hopefully. We were on the very edge of the hurricane, which is actually worse than being in the eye. Wind speeds can exceed a hundred miles an hour but the epicentre of a hurricane moves quite slowly. This one may be travelling at ten or fifteen knots and not in a straight line. So although it seems to be heading, like us, in the general direction of Florida, it is wavering from side to side and we may outstrip it."

"I'll tell you another advantage," she said.

"What's that?"

"In all the commotion I completely forgot to be seasick."

Two hours passed. Kathy seemed to be sleeping but I could not. It was warm but humid so our sodden clothes did not dry. Sinbad took a break, handing me the wheel. My orders were to continue driving our bow into the waves.

He lit a cigar and I watched him draw on it.

"Is that a twenty dollar Cohiba?"

He smiled and shook his head. I wondered how old he was. His face had a certain serenity – even resignation – that I had noticed before and I suspected he was older than he looked.

"How will things turn out in Cuba?" I asked. I felt bold enough after all we had been through to break a rule and talk about politics.

"I don't know," he said.

"What do you think of Communism?"

"The Castro version? I have mixed feelings. It is less corrupt than in other parts of the world, including Russia. Many Cubans are satisfied."

"Is that a compliment?"

He laughed. "Only up to a point. I was searching for something nice to say. Fidel is a colourful character and has been a major world influence, so Cubans are quite proud of that. On the other hand, he was a terrible manager and Raul is not much better. As a businessman myself, they make me cringe."

"Really?"

"To manage, you have to be able to listen and take advice. Fidel had too much ego. He preferred to follow his own ideas without listening to other people, including the experts. Do you know about his cattle breeding efforts?"

"No."

"He wanted to cross two strains, Brahman and Holstein, in hope of producing a new breed that would provide a national dairy herd and abundant milk for all. He lavished money and energy trying but the experiment was a complete flop. After fifty years we still don't have enough milk."

"Do you ever think of leaving?"

He examined the ash on his cigar. It was holding up well. "If I were just a fisherman I might consider it but, as you know, I am more than that. I do very well here. I take risks, but the 'fish' I catch are worth thousands of dollars each. Could I make the same money in Florida, and with expenses so low as to be almost non-existent?"

"I see your point."

"So I've come to terms with the fact that my father was tortured to death in a Castro prison."

It was hard to know what to say. "I'm sorry, I didn't really understand."

"They say the best revenge is to live well," he said without bitterness.

In a little while it began to get light. It had been a long night but in the mother-of-pearl dawn I could see the low profile of the Florida Keys, coming up out of the mist.

64

"WHERE EXACTLY ARE WE?" I asked Sinbad.

He pointed. "Coquina Key is over there. That's where Kon Feaver's cabin is."

"How in the world did you get it so accurate?"

"I've filled in for him before."

"Really? Kon works on a low-cost basis. I know he doesn't charge anywhere near the twelve grand going rate, so how do you handle that issue?"

Sinbad looked embarrassed but said nothing.

It was Kathy who got it. "You don't charge much either."

He shrugged. "It depends. I charge what people can afford to pay. Some passengers have well-heeled relatives in the United States."

"You're just a softie," she teased.

He cleared his throat and got busy with the compass and wheel.

As we drew close to land he asked Kathy, "Do you have your phone?"

She nodded. "I think I kept it dry."

"See if you can raise Kon."

She dialled. It rang for a long time but finally there was an answer.

"Good morning," she said. "Rise and shine."

The response must have been salty because she moved the phone away from her ear and grinned. "He sounds robust. The recovery must be going well."

I grabbed the phone. "How are you?"

"I'll know better when I've had some coffee. Where are you?"

"About ten minutes away."

"Don't come straight here, okay? I like to keep my place off the radar."

"Where, then?"

"There's a beach with an old jetty a couple of miles east along the Key. Nobody ever goes there. Sinbad knows it. I'll jump in the truck and be waiting for you."

Breakfast was a cheerful meal. We sat on the wooden deck outside Kon's home looking out over the Caribbean. His so-called cabin was much more than that. It was artfully camouflaged by palms and junipers that made it seem rustic and simple but, close up, it was a concrete block building with a steel roof that looked capable of withstanding even major hurricanes.

We ate scrambled eggs and bacon with hash browns, washed down with scalding coffee. I felt huge relief just to be back on U.S. soil again without the Cuban police to worry about.

Kathy downed a large glass of orange juice. "Thank God it's over."

"Is it?" I asked.

Kon and I looked at each other.

Kathy frowned. "What do you mean?"

"Hector Cruz is back in Cuba," I said carefully. He's in the past as far as we are concerned. But Stanley Rothman is still around, and here in the States. He's a mean, vindictive person and we frustrated his plans. That doesn't make me feel warm and safe."

"You're exaggerating. Lighten up," she said. She turned to Sinbad. "What about you?"

"I must be getting back."

"Back?"

He waved at the water to the south of us. There was thin sunshine and a patch of blue overhead, but there were grey skies in the distance.

"What's the forecast?" I asked Kon.

"The hurricane is still coming. People are starting to evacuate from the Keys, there are long lines of cars. The Governor has declared a state of emergency. Politicians are pretty gun-shy about that kind of thing nowadays, ever since Katrina killed more than a thousand Americans in '05 and made the head of FEMA and the U.S. President look like fools."

"Are we safe here?"

"Probably, but you never know. You would do better to drive north to the mainland."

I looked out at the ominous clouds. "You would be crazy to head into that mess," I said to Sinbad. "I know you're a fine sailor, but . . ."

"What else can I do? It's where I live."

"Why not stay in the States. 'Wet foot-dry foot' applies, so you can't be sent home. You are well and truly legal."

"I don't think Sinbad does 'legal,'" Kon grinned.

Sinbad nodded. "That's right. If my presence here became known I would be on the record forever. The Cuban authorities would know I had made it to the States. I would be finished."

"Finished?"

"I would have to stay here."

"Would that be so bad?" asked Kathy.

He turned an apologetic smile on her. "No disrespect, this is a fine country. But Cuba is my home."

Kon said, "At least hide out here for a few days or whatever it takes. Stay out of sight – I'll do your grocery shopping. When the weather improves, you can head home by the shortest possible route, saying hi to the sharks as you go."

"If you can accommodate me."

"As Ronald Reagan said, 'Mi casa es su casa.'"

Sinbad nodded. "Thank you."

Kathy got up. "I'm glad that's settled. I'm going to shower, do some laundry and sleep for twelve hours." She turned to Kon. "Now for the *really* important questions."

"Shoot."

"Do you have an iron and a hairdryer?"

"Of course."

"I'm impressed."

"You're not the first female to stay here," he said drily. "And I hope not the last."

"What about a clothes washer and dryer?"

He shook his head.

"How do you clean your clothes?"

I take them to the laundry in Marathon once a month."

She said nothing but her face said 'Men!' She rolled her eyes and disappeared into the bedroom.

When I followed her in, she had showered and

rinsed the salt out of her clothes in the tub. She was standing at the ironing board, wrapped in a towel, pressing the still damp garments. She had found some cologne somewhere and smelled delightful. I put my arms round her from behind and kissed the back of her neck and she snuggled against me. But we were both incredibly tired and we just collapsed on the bed in a heap. I don't know about her but I was asleep in seconds.

As we slept, Hurricane Matthew was flirting with the shores of Florida. The governors of Florida and South Carolina had already declared a state of emergency. Walt Disney World was closed. It was unclear which way Matthew would head next.

65

"THE HURRICANE MAY HAVE LOST interest in us," said Kon. He looked up at the morning sky, still leaden.

We stood on his deck. There was total silence, no hint of a breeze, the ocean flat as a millpond.

"It may zig or it may zag, there's no knowing. Best to head north while you still can."

So Kathy and I drove up from the Keys to my house in Coconut Grove. Just before we got there we stopped at Publix on Le Jeune and bought prefabricated sushi and a bottle of chilled Prosecco.

The house is small – two bedrooms and one bathroom, with a back yard full of fruit trees but no garage. My ten year old Subaru was standing in the dusty driveway, in need of a wash.

The rooms were still hot. The thermometer read 88°. The electricity was on – thank goodness I had remembered to pay the bill. I put the food in the fridge and set the air conditioning to 72 °.

Kathy wandered from room to room. Dirty dishes in the sink, un-matched socks on the floor. A bag of golf clubs in the hallway. In the bedroom twin fluorescent dots on the back of a firefly winked at us from a dark corner. She eyed the double bed. "Do you have such things as clean sheets?"

"Sheets, no problem. Clean? Let's see."

I rummaged in a closet and produced some rumpled sheets. I saw her gaze.

"They are clean, just not ironed," I said.

She wandered outside. I pointed out the mango, avocado and grapefruit trees.

"Cool." she said.

"For a Brit raised in cold weather, very."

"No pool."

"Can't have everything."

Indoors, we looked at each other as the firefly glowed in its corner. I think we both felt we had finally come through. We had fought the fight and made the grade. We were entitled to celebrate.

We undressed one another slowly and in silence but for the hum of the air conditioning as it cooled the small bedroom. Then we got under the covers and held each other for a few minutes without speaking. Finally she climbed on top of me and we made love, slowly at first and then with a vigour that felt like 'okay, go ahead without inhibition – you're back in the free world and there is nothing to be afraid of now.'

Later we were hungry. With enough Prosecco, Publix sushi really isn't all bad.

66

A FEW DAYS EARLIER, Stanley Rothman had received a call from Cruz.

"I need a transfer of funds," the policeman blurted.

"Calm down," said Rothman, irritated. "To which account?"

"I've opened a new bank account. The one in the Caymans was compromised."

"What do you mean by compromised?"

"Oliver Steele found out about it, so I opened a new account in Panama. I have the details for you."

Since the Russian income dried up Cruz had been burning through the money in his Cayman account. He had already skipped payments to a couple of lieutenants who were accustomed to receiving a monthly stipend and they had been quick to complain.

Rothman was in his penthouse office above the Strip eating a sandwich from Greenberg's Deli, corned beef on rye with plenty of mustard.

He was in the process of being sued for divorce and would need a very large amount of cash for that. At that moment he was pondering whether to exercise a hundred million dollars worth of stock options, so Cruz was small potatoes. But in Rothman's mind the Cuban was still part of the future, so he took the call.

When he was younger he had been fascinated by offshore tax havens and their convenient anonymity but nowadays he just declared a lot of income and paid a lot of tax. It was less risky and he liked to sleep at night.

It irritated him that Cruz would babble on about something that should only be mentioned very rarely. It showed a lack of sophistication and made him wonder, not for the first time, if Cruz was the right partner for him.

After returning from Havana, his impression of Hector Cruz was that he was a mixed bag. He was influential but he was also vain and obsessed with power. Stanley Rothman preferred to focus on money rather than power because, as he was fond of saying, power followed the dollar.

He still thought his best chance of getting a Cuban casino was to ally with Cruz but the policeman had screwed up, bungling the dossier business and losing ground to Martin Sanchez Madera at the same time.

The mention of Steele reminded him that the accountant was a persistent, annoying problem. Steele had the Cruz dossier. Having read it while he was with Mimi Tisch in Havana, Rothman knew how incriminating it was. It convinced him that Steele should be – he searched for the right word – neutralised. After a day or two pondering how to proceed and still unaware of Cruz's death, he picked up the phone. "Get me Frank Leon."

"Yes, Mr. Rothman."

"Not on the phone, in person. I want to see him."

Frankie Leon sat opposite Rothman.

"I want you to go to Florida for me."

Leon raised an eyebrow. "Interesting request. I'm not short of a buck, you know. I may not have your kind of money but I don't need to work."

"I understand, but I think this will appeal."

He pushed a photo across the desk. Leon glanced at it. "Oliver Steele."

"Your old pal."

Several years before, Frankie Leon had built up

an illegal gambling website on Antigua. Along the way he engaged in bribery, intimidation and murder. Steele, working for Carlton Tisch, had stripped control of it away from him. Leon had been forced to flee and go underground.

Since then he had rebranded himself from top to bottom with a new identity and passport and a lot of plastic surgery to face and body. He had drifted round the world in search of ways to make money quickly and fetched up in Las Vegas.

Rothman had enlisted his help in tapping the on-line gaming market, now legal. Leon was an expert who knew the business. Rothman had cut a few corners himself along the way so Leon's murky reputation didn't bother him.

Leon also loathed Oliver with a passion, correctly blaming him for his huge losses in Antigua.

"Where is he?" he gritted.

"He and a girlfriend were just seen in Miami – he has a house in Coconut Grove."

Franklin nodded. "I know the area."

Rothman explained the background. "I'm starting to think there's only one way out of this."

"What took you so long?"

Rothman shrugged. "I'm a bit too soft hearted."

"Want me to go down there and sort things out?" asked Leon.

"That may be the best way."

"I'll take that as a yes."

Rothman's Gulfstream carried Franklin to Miami. He caught a cab from the airport to a house he owned in Coral Gables. It was relatively modest – half a dozen bedrooms and bathrooms – in the upscale Cocoplum development just south of Coconut Grove.

He kept a bright red Jaguar F-Pace in the garage. He used it to make a run to the Publix on Monza Avenue. He bought a bottle of scotch and a steak – New York strip – which he took back and barbecued. He would take care of business in the morning.

Hurricane Matthew did brush the east coast of Florida on October 7th killing six people, but then it turned east and headed for the Bahamas. On Friday night it was downgraded to a Category Two storm which went on to hit Georgia and the Carolinas. In North Carolina, nearly 900 people had to be rescued from their flooded homes by boat crews. In all, the storm left over a million homeless and killed 47 people in the United States. Damage was estimated at $10 billion.

I CALLED CARLTON TISCH. "I'm home and so is Kathy. What about Mimi?"

"She got back last night."

"Safe and well, I hope?"

Yes. If you want to be paid, send me a bill for your services."

"Will do."

That's Carlton, all heart.

"How about brunch at Trainer's Raw Bar on Bayshore?" I suggested to Kathy.

"Sounds like a plan."

Monty Trainers is more commercial than in the old days. Some say it lost its soul somewhere along the way but it still has a great view past Dinner Key towards Key Biscayne.

It was a sunny morning and all seemed right with the world. Jimmy Buffett's "Volcano" was playing and you half expected Jimmy to drop by for a cheeseburger.

We ordered a fry-up of clams, shrimp and calamari and dunked the golden morsels in tartare sauce. She watched me eat with my fingers. "You handle that well for a limey."

"I'm a bit of both." I divided the remaining clams into two equal piles and pushed one of them toward her.

Her lip curled in scorn. "Accountant!"

"Guilty," I said.

"I feel like a swim," said Kathy later. She stretched lazily.

"Why not. We can go to the Venetian Pool."

"What's that?"

"You'll see."

We swung by the house to pick up swimsuits, then drove north on Le Jeune, turned left into Coral Gables and came to rest outside a Spanish style building with a pink tiled roof.

"What's this?"

"This is the Venetian Pool. It's the municipal

swimming pool of Coral Gables, adapted from an old rock quarry. It's also the largest freshwater pool in the United States."

We paid and went in.

The style was part Italian, part Spanish, part Floridian. An ornamental bridge led to an island in the middle of the pool with two full sized palm trees. Across from the island was a huge waterfall and a coral grotto with rocky caves stretching back into the hillside. There was a café with food and a sandy beach area.

"This is amazing," said Kathy, eying the rocky waterfall fifty yards away across the huge pool. "Is this place really natural?"

"Pretty much. It was carved out of the rock in the 1920's and draws its water from natural artesian wells."

"I love it."

"It's spring water, very clean," I explained. "They used to empty and refill it nightly but that made such heavy demands on the Florida water table that now they just flow it back into the aquifer through natural ground filtration."

"Well it's just what I need." She disappeared in the direction of the changing rooms and reappeared bikini-clad a few minutes later.

We dived in and splashed over to a rocky grotto that seemed to be hewn by nature out of the rock. It provided welcome shade from the still-powerful afternoon sun.

There were plenty of bathers around but my attention was caught particularly by a pale skinned man in his forties swimming some distance away. Once or twice he seemed to be looking at us but then he swam away and I thought no more about it.

"It's really hot, let's get a drink," said Kathy.

We bought sodas at the kiosk and went and spread our towels on the sand and let the sun beat on our bodies.

"You're a sun freak," she said.

"Where did you get that bikini?" I asked. It was navy blue and very smart.

"I'm never without one. It was in the car when I drove you from Cayo Santa Maria to Caibarian."

"You look great," I said. She knows I'm a fan but I make it a point to say that kind of thing. Like saying sorry, it never hurts.

She laughed. "Thanks. No topless action here I suppose?"

"Right." Out of the corner of my eye, I glimpsed that bather again. He didn't look quite right but I didn't say anything.

"You know I feel better here than on Cayo Santa Maria," she said. "The Magnifica was a grand hotel and this is only a public pool, but even so."

I nodded. "Somehow the Magnifica isn't Cuba."

"I keep thinking of those pathetic ration books while we were feeding our faces at the buffet and swigging imported wine."

The sunshine was nice but I couldn't help noticing the same guy again. He was at the edge of my field of vision but he was there. I had left my Beretta in the car's glove box. I sort of regretted that. But I told myself not to fuss. I was worrying unduly, seeing imaginary threats.

I looked at my watch. "Had enough sun? Back to the house, get cleaned up, then out to La Carreta for *ropa vieja* with black beans and rice?"

"Works for me."

As we began the drive home I took the Beretta out of the glove compartment and slipped it into my pocket. Kathy raised her eyebrows but said nothing.

In the house, she went to change. I did too, but it didn't take me long. I was in the living room switching on the television when I glimpsed a shadow on the opposite wall. I reached for my pistol and crouched down on the floor.

A fusillade of silenced shots sprayed the living room. Bullet holes peppered the wall above my head.

I waited.

Silence for a full minute except for the noise of the bathroom shower. Then the shadow crept slowly across the wall as its owner moved into the hallway.

68

"I CAN SEE YOU," I said pleasantly.

The shadow disappeared.

I inched through the door cautiously, or so I thought. But as I breasted the doorway, gun arm extended, a club-like object descended on my fingers with painful force and knocked the weapon out of my hand. It clattered to the floor.

I crouched on one knee to pick it up.

"Best let it lie," said the man. His pasty face beneath a shock of blonde hair split in a crooked smile. One hand held the putter from my golf bag. In the other, a pistol trained at my chest. He looked comfortable with it although frankly at that range nobody could miss.

I stood up. "I saw you at the pool."

"Yeah, I was careless. Doesn't matter now, though."

A Brooklyn twang. I had a feeling I had seen him before. "Who are you?"

"Name is Larry Franklin."

I didn't recognise the name at first, but then the penny dropped.

"You were partners with Kalestian in the Macau Excelsior!"

"Briefly. He bought me out."

Events replayed in my mind. Franklin had appeared from nowhere last year when Michael Kalestian had been desperate for money to complete his casino in Macau and had signed a very advantageous loan agreement with the impetuous Armenian-American. But what the hell was he doing here?

He saw my confusion and laughed. "I live in Vegas now. We have a mutual friend, Stanley Rothman."

Not good news. Things were becoming clearer, although I still didn't understand his connection with the elderly magnate.

He went on. "Stanley consults me on various matters. He says you are causing him problems in Cuba. Long story short, he decided you must be disposed of."

I inched round towards the window, shaking my head. "Sorry, a bit dizzy. Need air."

It didn't fool Franklin. His gun followed me round.

"I still don't understand," I said. "You said you were a consultant. Why would you come all this way and get involved in the violent stuff?"

The crooked smile again. "My name is Larry Franklin now but you may remember me as Frankie Leon."

Sometimes in life one's view suddenly expands. You see your whole history as a continuum of past and present, dotted with highlights. I felt like that now.

Early in my time with Carlton, he sent me to Antigua to deal with this unpleasant character Frankie Leon who owned a gaming website. Leon was ruthlessly dunning an old pal of Carlton's who had a gambling addiction. Bottom lime: Leon lost a billion dollar business thanks to me, and then had to disappear to avoid a murder charge.

Now he was back. And very bitter. Rothman had chosen his man well.

Looking closer I could see that it was indeed Leon under all the surgery. The nose and lips had changed, and the hair colour. But other things – the height, the squirrely eyes that wouldn't meet mine – were the same. And that accent.

He smiled. "Time to say goodbye."

I thought of a dozen smart ways to talk him

round but it was too late because he raised his aim from my stomach to my chest. He was close enough that I could see his finger tightening.

The silenced report was not deafening but it shook the small house.

Kathy stood in the doorway holding my gun, which she had scooped up from the floor. Her face was dead white.

"Nice," I said.

She was shaking.

"Your first time?"

She nodded. "I thought there would be a recoil. I held it tight, to allow for that."

"You did well. What can I say?"

"How about 'thank you?'"

A hug seemed in order, which she returned.

She indicated the body. "What shall we do with that?"

I checked for a pulse but he was well and truly dead.

"No problem." I retrieved my phone and dialled 911.

"I want to report a home invasion."

69

CALEB WAS on his way to a concert.

It was the second time in a few days, but this time he sensed things were for real.

The call had come just hours before, from the *Orquestra Buena Vista Social Club*, a big name in Havana. He suspected he was a late substitute but he was not too proud to accept.

The venue was impressive. The Palacio de la Marquesa de Villalba was an immense 19th Century grey building the size of a city block with classic arches the length of the building. Like most of Havana it had weathered but in this case gracefully thanks to its massive construction.

The *Orquestra* represented a fabled piece of Cuban history. In the 1940s the Buena Vista Social

Club was for musicians to get together and perform or socialise. In the nineties a U.S. guitarist, Ry Cooder, went to Havana and recorded members of the original club, most of whom were by then in their seventies. The album was a huge international success.

No good deed goes unpunished. Cooder was prosecuted in the United States for violating the embargo and fined $25,000. But Cuban music was reintroduced to fans around the world who were delighted by the nostalgic tribute to a vanished era. There are now many clubs in Havana where visitors can go to hear the old-style music. The Orquestra Buena Vista Social Club was prominent and it seemed Caleb was to have a chance of singing with them.

Following instructions, he walked up broad stone steps to the second floor where he was greeted by an attractive young woman who explained the situation.

"How did I get chosen?"

"Martin Sanchez Madera at the University mentioned you to our Director. One of our tenors called in sick this morning, so we phoned you."

He looked around. This was once the home of a single noble family, yet it was huge. Nobody lives like that now, he thought. Or did they? There were stories about Fidel. Great ranches that were said to be his residences although for security he moved from place to place at short notice.

The music director called the group together.

"We have a new member this evening." He smiled at Caleb and there were murmured greetings.

Caleb knew the playlist by heart. The man he was replacing sang mostly group parts but also a solo, '*Candela*.'

"Carlos here also does *Candela*, or we could use you. Want to give it a try?"

Caleb complied:

"Ay Candela, Candela, Candela me quemo aé
    Margarita llama pronto a los bomberos
    para que vengan a apagar el fuego"

Oh fire, fire, fire I'm burning oh
    Margarita call the firefighters soon
    so they come to put out the fire

He gave a decent account of the song, his voice strong and expressive. The director nodded. Caleb noticed Carlos frowning and wondered if he had made an enemy.

· · ·

The audience arrived, climbing the broad stairs up into the cavernous hall.

Expectation built as the house lights dimmed, stage lights clicked on. The band played the opening chords and the singers faced the audience. Mostly male, middle aged, in jackets and ties. One in pale blue, one scarlet, one cloth of gold. Others, like Caleb, were in black. All wore caps or hats. Their faces were every hue from pale white to jet black, each line and wrinkle picked out in the glare.

The band was large: five trumpets, a keyboard, maracas, clavos, the gourd-like güiro, cello and a young girl gyrating, eye candy. The music was nonstop, starting strong and getting stronger. The singers' rapport with a delighted audience raised the atmosphere to fever pitch.

Eventually they came to *Candela*. Caleb smiled and gave it his best. The audience cheered loudly.

A young black dancer with broad shoulders and narrow waist leaped onto the floor. He wore black – silk open shirt and waistcoat, hair drawn back in a ponytail, energetic moves, a dramatic somersault now and again but mostly moving his hips sinuously and raising his arms to get the audience to clap in time.

He beckoned a pretty girl sitting with a male companion and dragged her, reluctant, onto the floor. In no time she was dancing the salsa. He twirled her around, then added more women in a conga line threading through the narrow gaps between tables.

The evening ended with *Guantánamera*.

The iconic song about a young woman from Guantánamo, the province better known in the United States for its military base, evokes the spirit of Cuba. The song uses lines by José Marti, hero of the 1895 War of Independence from Spain.

Each singer sang a verse. Caleb was not sure whether he would be included but Carlos, who was next-to-last, sang and then with a nod handed him the microphone.

He sang:

"Yo soy un hombre sincero, de donde crece la palma

Y antes de morir yo quiero cantar mis versos del alma"

I am a truehearted man, who comes from where the palm trees grow,

Before I lay down my life, I long to coin the verses of my soul.

. . .

then raised his fist, punched the air and shouted "Que viva Cuba."

70

FIDEL CASTRO DIED a few weeks later, on November 25th, 2016.

Outside Versailles Restaurant on Miami's Calle Ocho, jubilant demonstrators carried signs saying "Satan, Fidel is now yours."

But there was real grief among huge numbers of Cubans. His ashes were put on a ceremonial carriage which travelled across the country from Havana back to a funeral in Santiago de Cuba in the east, reversing the route he took after his revolutionary triumph 57 years before.

A young Cuban woman told CNN, "The Cuban people are feeling sad because of the loss of our commander in chief Fidel Castro Ruz, and we wish him, wherever he is, that he is blessed, and us Cubans love him."

President Barack Obama who had visited Cuba earlier in 2016 extended "a hand of friendship to the Cuban people" as he offered his condolences to Castro's family.

Pope Francis sent a telegram to Raul Castro expressing his sorrow for Castro's family and the Cuban people and offering his prayers.

US Congresswoman Ileana Ros-Lehtinen, the first Cuban-American elected to Congress, cautioned that "the death of one dictator will not usher a new wave of change because the rulers of Cuba, whether it's Fidel, Raul, whatever names you give them, they just rule over Cuba with an iron fist."

In January 2017, a week before leaving office, outgoing President Obama announced an end to the "wet foot-dry foot" immigration policy.

Mid-way through 2017, President Trump again imposed restrictions on travel and business with Cuba.

Casino owner Stanley Rothman was furious. He was already puzzled by the lack of communication from Hector Cruz and the fact that he had not been asked for money recently made him wonder if the Cienfuegos police chief was dead or in prison. Under Trump's new rules, Rothman would apparently not even be allowed to manage a Cuban hotel, let alone own a casino. A major contributor to the Republican election campaign, and this was the thanks he got? He immediately ceased contributing to Republican campaigns.

Every cloud has a silver lining. Bruno saw his business in black market consumer goods go from strength to strength as tourist dollars continued to flow from Canada, Europe and South America into the hands of the Cuban few.

Cuba's Foreign Minister observed that the regime had survived half a century of U.S. embargo and would continue to do so.

If anyone thought differently they were smoking the wrong brand of cigar.

THE END

Now read on for a sneak peek at the next *Oliver Steele and Kon Feaver* thriller, **FEAVER PITCH**:

Chapter 1

Kon? This Is Pedro. It's about Bruno. It's bad news."

I usually screen calls when I'm at home at my cabin on Coquina Key but Pedro is someone I trust, so when I heard his voice on the speaker I took this one.

I picked up the phone. "What?"

"He's been shot. He's dead, Kon."

It took me a moment to react. Bruno Pérez was the closest thing I had to a best friend. But death, alas, is something I am very familiar with. Years ago, I was a fighter pilot in the Israeli Air Force, although they fired me after a year for being drunk most of the time. I've had a bumpy career since then, first as a mercenary in Africa and then as a small-time drug dealer in Miami. But nowadays, despite ferrying refugees from Cuba to Florida which is what I do for a living, my life is mostly non-violent.

"What happened?"

"I don't know. I came round to take him to breakfast as we arranged last night when we met at a party on Star Island, and found his body."

"Have you called the police?"

"I'm about to."

"But you called me first?"

"Yes."

We both knew why. The three of us had history.

Last year I very nearly died in Cuba. In the course of a boat run I was arrested on a beach near Havana, taken to a prison island and locked in a cage for three days without food or much hope of surviving. Pedro and Bruno, along with my well-spoken English friend Oliver Steele, rescued me. Afterwards Bruno, not surprisingly, found it prudent to leave Cuba. He now lives – or lived – in Coral Gables, a decent but not grand suburb of Miami.

It was at least possible that Bruno's death had to do with enemies he made during that episode. Either way, Pedro and I would have strong opinions about what should be done to his killer.

"I'll come round," I said.

"How long?"

"About an hour. Must you call the police?"

"I think so, but not right away. They don't know what time I got here so they won't know how long I waited before phoning them." Pedro lives in Hialeah, ten miles north of Coral Gables, along with many other second and third generation Cuban Americans.

"I hear you."

I got into my '97 Jeep Grand Cherokee V8, bright red with gold trim. I started the engine, stopped and thought. I got out, went back into the house, fetched the Glock 19 from the kitchen drawer and shoved it in my pants pocket, then headed up the road.

Chapter 2

With my foot down hard I made it to Coral Gables in forty minutes. I love the Jeep dearly, but it's an electricity hog and if I don't use it almost daily the battery goes flat, so it welcomed the mileage.

Bruno's apartment was on the second floor of a down-at-heel two storey building of a dozen units, a couple of blocks south of the glitzy Cuban diner Versailles. The downstairs entrance to the once-white structure boasted a lock but it was broken, so I pushed my way in and climbed uncarpeted concrete stairs. Without air conditioning the atmosphere was damp and muggy, typical Miami in August.

The flat was a small one-bedroom but at least it was cool. In the narrow hallway Pedro greeted me, looking grim. "In there." He pointed to the living room.

Bruno's slim body lay on its back on the floor. His pale torso wore black boxer shorts and a blood-stained towelling robe. He had been shot several times. Proximate cause of death was a through-and-through hole in the middle of his chest, barely a trickle of blood in front, but behind, a mess of blood and human tissue, spread in a pool on the worn carpet. Some of the blood had spattered an open newspaper, yesterday's *Miami Herald*, that lay partly underneath the body.

But it was the other wounds that shocked me. A

bullet in each knee, neither of them fatal but both unimaginably painful, showing sadism by the killer. A choice had apparently been made not just to end the young man's life, but to inflict maximum suffering.

Probably to make a point, too – for the minutes or hours it took to snuff out his life. The shooter wanted Bruno not just to know his killer but to acknowledge, through a haze of agony, why he was being killed. For that, one knee would have been enough. As for the second knee, what sort of sadist would do that? What did he say to Bruno between the first and the second bullet? That he was going to double the punishment, ratchet up the pain? Such sadistic behaviour suggested the worst kind of human predator.

I looked at Pedro, who nodded. Hard to describe how I felt at that moment, but quiet fury about covers it.

I owed Bruno a lot. My arrest occurred just as I was about to run a boatload of refugees back to the States. It's a service I still provide despite some political changes since then. Things have quietened down a bit in that department since the death of Fidel Castro. President Obama ended 'Wet foot-dry foot' the following year. Fidel's brother Raúl, who succeeded him as President, gave way to Miguel Díaz-Canel, although Raúl is chief secretary of the communist party; in other words he's still the boss. Díaz-Canel, who is a lot younger, is a canny politician who may show more liberal behaviour one day, but for now he's concentrating on not offending the powers that be, i.e. not getting fired. Meanwhile, most Cubans are still dirt poor. Many still want to leave and have enough relatives in Florida willing to pay my fees that I stay in business.

Anyway, I was taken to a prison island off the south coast of Cuba and locked in a cage four feet square and three feet high. I was there for three days and suffered the worst pain I've ever experienced.

They were trying to get me to explain why Martin Sanchez-Madera, an opposition political figure, was on my boat. The problem was, I had no idea. He was just a passenger, one of twenty. I couldn't tell them something I didn't know. I would almost certainly have died in that cage.

So, heartfelt thanks to my friend Oliver who enlisted Bruno, my contact in Havana. That in turn led to Pedro sending a helicopter full of anti-Castro freedom fighters to rescue me.

"You were together at a party last night?" I asked.

"Yes."

"Could that have something to do with this?"

"Maybe."

"What sort of party?"

"It was on Star Island."

"The high rent district, eh?"

"Yep."

"Where exactly?"

"At Stanley Rothman's place."

I formed a mental picture of Rothman, a short, bald businessman in his seventies with a permanent unfriendly smirk.

"Really! Are you party-going buddies with Mr. Rothman?"

Who is Stanley Rothman? He's the owner of the huge Portofino Resort in Las Vegas and its even bigger counterpart in Macau. So he is very rich. He's also a nasty piece of work. He tried to open a casino in Havana a couple of years ago by bribing Hector Cruz, a crooked police chief and would-be next president of Cuba. That didn't work out – Cruz came to a sticky end one dark night at the hands of my friend Oliver. Besides that, one of Donald Trump's first actions on becoming president was to tighten the rules against US investment in Cuba that Obama had relaxed.

Pedro looked embarrassed. "No, but I admit I was curious to see his place on the island."

I would have been curious too. You don't buy a home on that man-made rock unless you are really in the chips. Star Island was built by the Army Corps of Engineers in the 1920s and sits in Biscayne Bay, connected to the mainland by a narrow causeway.

Movie stars, athletes and wealthy financiers like Rothman live there. It's the polar opposite of my own little island, Coquina Key, which is home mostly to layabouts like me.

"Okay," I said. "We'll gloss over that. Who else was invited?"

"Hannah Mann, who is a good looking doctor from South Beach. Our mutual friend Martin Sanchez-Madera. The rock singer Rod Stirling. Bruno of course. And a couple of British females called Emma and Courtney Watts. Twins."

"That's it?"

"Yeah."

"So apart from you and Bruno, just six people. A select group."

"You could say so."

"Why did Rothman invite them? Not because they were his close friends, I shouldn't think."

In Cuba, Rothman had been on the opposite side from me and my pals. He got involved because, in pursuit of his casino ambitions, he was cultivating Cruz, the cop who kidnapped me.

As for the others: Martin Sanchez-Madera was the anti-Castro intellectual who Cruz had tried to snatch off my boat. He was later imprisoned and would no doubt have been killed if Oliver hadn't blackmailed and then shot Cruz. Soon afterwards, Martin found life in Havana too hot for comfort and, like Bruno, escaped to Miami, deeming survival to be the better part of valour.

"Rod Stirling was probably only there because Rothman is a snob and likes famous names," I said.

Stirling was a household name in the music industry, but by no means an ornament. He had a string of convictions for drug possession, GBH against female fans and tax evasion in the United States, Britain and, for some strange reason, Monaco. Whoever heard of Monaco suing anyone for tax evasion? I didn't know they had any. Taxes, that is. But apparently he lied on his application for residence. All I knew about him was that when a girlfriend took me to a Stirling concert, he arrived an hour late and as high as a kite.

"You may be right," said Pedro. "Martin and I were probably there because Rothman hasn't given up on the Havana casino. He's the sort of guy who likes to keep his friends close and his enemies closer."

"In case they could be useful one day?"

"Exactly."

"What about the women?"

Pedro shrugged. "Hannah Mann is his doctor. The Watts twins may just have been eye candy – their father was a wealthy stockbroker on Antigua."

"Do you think anyone there had it in for Bruno?"

"Rothman himself, maybe. As for the others, I have no way of knowing."

"What did you all talk about?"

"Politics, sports, things like that."

"Sounds pretty blah."

"Really. I was only there a couple of hours, then I split."

I was thinking I should investigate each of the guests. I owed Bruno that. I said so to Pedro.

He looked doubtful. "Don't do anything rash."

"Of course not. Except to cut the heart out of whoever did this." I indicated the body.

He shook his head, warning. I remembered that among other things he was a deputy sheriff in Hialeah.

Pedro is my age, thirty-eight. Although born in Florida, he's Cuban on both sides, the grandson of Hugo Macias, a pillar of the Cuban-American community. Hugo was a colleague of Fidel Castro in the early days, before Fidel's communist tendencies became apparent. After speaking out critically a number of times he was arrested, convicted of betraying the revolution – Fidel's standard charge – and imprisoned for ten years in one of the vast circular penal towers on Isla de Pinos. Finally released, he escaped to Florida where he became an honoured figure among the Cuban population. Now in his nineties, he is more or less retired from public life, but his grandson Pedro carries on his legacy on behalf of émigrés hoping to return.

Pedro is a complex personality who has put his own stamp on the position. He manages to be a respected public figure – hence the deputy sheriff handle – but at the same time the leader of a secret militia of counter-revolutionaries that train at hidden locations in the Everglades, in preparation for the day when they will sweep back to power in Cuba, over the cold dead limbs of the regime.

Rothman would be aware of this, of course. No doubt in his twisted way he hoped to use the acquaintanceship to further his casino ambitions one day, on the principle that 'the enemy of my enemy is my friend.'

That I could understand. But for Rothman to cultivate Bruno was harder to figure.

Pedro looked at his watch. "Time to call the cops."

I shrugged. "I guess so. Will you call Hialeah PD? I know you're a deputy sheriff there."

He shook his head. "No, Miami-Dade. This is serious stuff. And when they arrive, remember we only just got here."

To their credit, the police arrived in five minutes, a pair, both in their thirties.

Lieutenant Oliveira was maybe thirty, Hispanic, handsome, hair glossy black, skin the colour of her name. She wore plain clothes, at least I assume that's what they were – form-fitting navy pants, white shirt on the tight side with the upper buttons undone, no badges.

Her sergeant companion was called Taylor, according to the tag on his khaki shirt. Hefty belt, bulging holster in polished leather you could see your face in. A scowl. Didn't like playing second banana to a woman, was my guess. Red face, pale skin, his bullet head covered in a tight cowl of ginger hair. He would always have a problem with sunburn in these latitudes.

Oliveira took in the scene, including the body, at a glance. She turned to Pedro. "Who is he?"

"His name is Bruno Pérez, he's a recent immigrant from Cuba. Last year, anyway."

She knelt down and leaned closer to the body. Parts of the newspaper under Bruno's left arm were soaked with blood. I had not noticed before, but the tip of the index finger of his other hand was also bloodstained, as if had been dipped in red ink. A red mark on the newspaper, if you used your imagination freely, might have described the shape of a crude, five pointed star. The points were not regular, although it was a good effort for a dying man. But it was certainly not obvious, at least not to Oliveira, who shrugged and stood up.

She turned to Pedro again. "How do you come to be here?"

"He's a friend. We were going to have breakfast. I came to pick him up."

'From Hialeah?"

"Yes. I'm an honorary deputy sheriff there." He produced an ID card which she waved away.

"I know who you are, and your family."

"Are you Cuban?" asked Pedro.

"Both parents, yes."

Taylor was staring at me. Suspiciously I thought, but maybe it was his natural expression.

"What about you?"

"What about me?"

"Why are you here?"

"I'm another friend."

"He was in the area," said Pedro.

Taylor seemed to have taken a dislike to me. "What's your name?" he asked.

"Feaver. Kon Feaver."

"What kind of name is that?"

"It's Israeli."

"You Jewish?"

"Israeli."

He looked puzzled and turned to the corpse, studying it as he put on rubber gloves. Feeling around in the pool of bloody matter under Bruno's legs, he got hold of a bullet and held it up.

"Looks like a .38." He stood up. "Are either of you armed?"

Pedro shook his head. I did not.

"Well?" Taylor asked, still looking at me.

Nothing else for it. I produced the Glock. "Different bullets, 9mm. And not fired."

"I wasn't implying anything," he said.

The hell he wasn't. "Of course not," I said.

"You usually walk around armed?"

"Depends how I feel."

"Got a permit?"

I reached in my wallet and produced a dog-eared, much-folded sheet of paper which he held close to his nose. Short sighted but too vain to wear glasses? "This is not the original."

"It's a copy. I keep it to show folk like you."

He sniffed and gave it back.

"We have to process the scene," said Oliveira briskly. She nodded at me. "Leave us your particulars."

Which I did.

I took a last look at the body of Bruno with its ravaged knees.

Then I set out to find his killer.

Chapter 3

It was not yet noon as I headed for Star Island.

I had no evidence that Bruno's death was in any way connected to Stanley Rothman's party the night before. But I had no leads and nothing to go on, apart from that mark on the newspaper. It was a place to start.

I drove out on MacArthur Causeway and stopped at the Star Island gatehouse where I was inspected by an overweight guard in safari jacket and reflector sunglasses. He frowned at my dusty Jeep.

"What's your business?"

"It's personal," I said and smiled.

"These are private homes."

"But it's a public road," I said.

He scowled. He walked round the Jeep and photographed the number plate with his mobile phone. I drove in.

Star Island is for the rich – actually, the very rich – and the glitzy in showbusiness, finance and sports. Or anyone else with money. Lots of it. A house with ten bedrooms there is nothing.

You can see many of the homes at their best from the ocean. Rothman's place was a white, many-pillared mansion with a huge pool, liberally dressed with tall palms and colourful bougainvillea, but from the road all I could see was fifty yards of high white wall, split in the middle by another gatehouse. Either Star Island folk were obsessed with security or they just liked to show off. No human being here, just a camera, a microphone and a buzzer, which I pressed.

"Yes?" A female voice.

"Here to see Mr. Rothman."

"Who are you?"

"Kon Feaver."

"Do you have an appointment?"

"No."

"Does he know you?"

"He should."

"What's it about?"

"That's enough. Tell him I'm here."

"Just a minute."

She came back. "He'll see you." She didn't sound happy, but the white painted boom swung up and I was in.

He was standing out on a long white marble-paved terrace, facing the ocean but glassed-in and air conditioned to 72 degrees. I approached. He did not offer to shake hands.

We had never met but we knew about each other. When Pedro and his troops rescued me from the prison island, it had been necessary for Oliver Steele to shoot the police chief of Santa Clara province, Hector Cruz. This was the same Cruz to whom

Rothman paid a couple of million bucks in the hope of gaining a casino concession. Small change for a billionaire, but enough for him to view me with serious hostility, since I had been prominent in screwing up his plans. As we stood face to face now, that may have been on both our minds.

"I'm quite busy," he said.

He was in his seventies, short, a few wisps of ginger hair left. Not a nice face, smooth and fleshy, the mouth turned down, the eyes narrow and calculating. He wore a grey jacket, , and a white shirt and tie, the jacket one-buttoned across a prominent belly. He looked overdressed for Miami in August. Feeling the cold?

I said, "It's about Bruno Pérez."

He nodded. "He was here yesterday."

"He's dead," I said.

A flicker of the eyes. Surprise. But was it surprise that Bruno was dead, or surprise that I knew he was dead?

"What happened?"

"He was shot. Kneecapped in both legs, then shot in the chest."

"That's awful," he said.

"You had a party here last night," I said.

A mask came down. Almost imperceptibly, but I noticed.

"What of it?"

"Including several Cubans."

"Yes."

"Why?"

"Why not?"

"You didn't invite me," I said.

He looked me up and down. I got the impression that if I'd been a palmetto bug he would have squashed me underfoot. I could see I wasn't going to get much help.

"I know who you are, but you are not relevant to my plans for Cuba," he said.

"Which plans?"

"You know very well. They haven't changed."

"Was that the reason for the party? You were just keeping in touch with people who might one day help you?"

"Exactly.

"But Bruno would never help you, considering how you treated each other." Bruno's efforts had led to Rothman being forced to abandon his Cuban ambitions, at least temporarily.

Rothman gave the slightest of shrugs. It could have meant, "Yes but one never knows," or "Yes but I thought I could bribe him to change his mind." Or, "Yes so I had him killed."

I heard a voice behind me. "Why don't you throw the jerk out, Stan?"

I turned. The face was familiar. It was thin, fox

like and pimpled, the voice gravelly, the whole package bereft of empathy. Rod Stirling, none other, veteran of a thousand concerts and TV screens.

I walked towards him. I don't control my temper as well as I should. I can't help it. It's a trait that made me a successful athlete when I was younger – including playing goalkeeper for Tel Aviv – but it does get me into a lot of trouble, and that included now. I stopped when my face was a foot from his.

"You were saying?" I asked.

Stirling didn't back away. He was tall and skinny, about my age, an amused smirk on his face. No physical coward, then.

"You don't look like you belong here," he said.

"And you do? How's that?"

"How's that? I guess it's about money," he said.

"Which you have?"

"Enough to buy you out a hundred times."

"Well whoopidoo," I said.

He looked me up and down. I was in the clothes I wear every day in the Keys, faded jeans and a navy polo shirt because it doesn't show the dirt, so I suppose I didn't look very smart. I'm seriously suntanned, not a fancy pool-side tan, more the kind you get from working on a wooden deck, painting the cabin, fishing, gardening and all around exposure to the glare of the sun that bleaches the Conch Republic. Add matted black hair and two days worth of stubble and I suppose I could be mistaken for a penniless Latino day labourer.

"What's your name?" he asked.

"Feaver."

"What kind of name is that?"

"It's an anglicisation of Feinberg."

"You Jewish?"

"Israeli."

Stanley Rothman held up a hand as if to stop teenage kids arguing. "Mr. Feaver brought me some bad news," he said. "Bruno Pérez is dead."

I was watching Stirling's face. No reaction. He didn't blink, literally or metaphorically. I wondered if he was stoned.

"Bruno who?" asked Stirling.

"The man that was here last night."

"The small time Cuban wheeler-dealer?"

I didn't like the characterisation but it was basically true. Bruno made a living importing US consumer goods, toasters and microwaves, to Havana and selling them on the black market at a huge markup. Last year he quit Cuba because the pressure was on, thanks to his helping me get out of jail. Now he ran the same business from Miami, dealing with a cousin in Havana and another man in Santiago de Cuba. I assume he was making good money.

I turned to Rothman. "To the point," I said. "Do

either of you have any idea who would have killed Bruno?"

Rothman shook his head. "A business enemy perhaps?"

I had to admit it was possible. Bruno's business ethics were elastic and he could have pissed off any number of suppliers to whom he owed money. Customers not so much, since he invariably demanded payment in advance.

Stirling chose to take my question personally. He swayed closer – he was definitely high on something, barely in control of his limbs. "You calling one of us a murderer?" he said.

"If the cap fits."

He drew back an arm and swung at me. I didn't think he could do me much harm so I barely moved, and his fist grazed my cheek. There was a gold ring on his finger and it broke the skin. The sting was sharp.

I guess I was humiliated that he made contact. Anyway, I snapped. I punched him hard on the nose and he went down like a log, collapsing on the white marble. There was quite a lot of blood. I stepped back, embarrassed, and turned to Rothman.

"I don't rate your taste in friends," I said.

He was as surprised as I was and said nothing.

I shrugged and turned to leave. The atmosphere

had gone downhill and there didn't seem much point in staying.

On the outward lane through the gatehouse there was another wooden crossbar. The way I felt, I was prepared to smash through it, but luckily it was on some kind of automatic switch and it rose as the Jeep approached.

So much for Star Island. Time to try my luck with another party guest.

Something less violent seemed in order. I decided on Doctor Hannah Mann.

Chapter 4

I googled Hannah Mann on my iPhone and found a listing for *H. Mann, MD Inc.* with an address on Brickell, downtown Miami's main drag.

I toyed with the idea of calling ahead and making an appointment. My unannounced meeting with Stanley Rothman had ended in violence, after all. Then I thought, well maybe not. That meeting had taught me quite a bit about Rothman and his unlovable pal Stirling. And to be honest, I sort of enjoyed the confrontation. The same approach might work again. So I decided to forge ahead.

More precisely, when I got to her building I took the Jeep to the 36th floor. Yes, you heard right, there was no parking on the street. I just drove the automobile onto something called the 'Vehicle Elevator,' pressed a button and up I went, car and all.

I'd read about these ultra-expensive towers where your ride occupies a garage on the same floor as your apartment, but this was the first time I had been in one. It was an eerie, weightless feeling. My first thought was the expense – it must be costing someone an arm and a leg.

At the 36th floor I got out of the Jeep and found myself facing a glass wall with a door that slid silently back to reveal a lobby and a male receptionist behind a long glass desk. Behind him, a floor-to-ceiling window looked out across blue ocean and farther away the green vegetation of Key Biscayne. The general impression was of light and space.

The man behind the desk was slim, smiling and completely bald. And erotic. I am not into the gay thing, personally. Ever since I began to take an interest in sex I've preferred women. To each his own, I guess. He had an aura though, no doubt about it. Maybe it was the maroon paisley silk shirt open to the waist over a smooth tanned chest, or the vee shaped torso and small buns in tight white pants.

He smiled agreeably.

"Is the doctor in?" I asked.

People sometimes lie or are at least evasive when asked that question. They say something along the lines of she's "in a meeting" or "not available." But not a bit of it, the smile widened.

"Sure, Mr. Kon Feaver," he said with a faint accent. Most accents you hear in Miami are Latino or Hispanic or whatever term you want to use. People call it the capital of South America. But this accent was different, more European.

"Have we met?" I asked. "How do you know my name?"

He laughed. "Pedro Macias vouched for you."

"What do you mean, 'vouched?'"

"He said you would be getting in touch."

That darned Pedro. My chain of thought was

interrupted by the appearance in the doorway of a woman who had to be Hannah.

She too was smiling. "Hi Kon!" she said to me, and to him, "Hold my calls, Rudi."

So, German? She beckoned me into her office.

I should be so lucky, to have such a doctor. Blonde, five foot seven or eight, curved in the right places, in a knitted yellow silk dress that fit like paint. And she seemed genuinely pleased to see me. You know how sometimes at a party you'll see a woman across the room who you'd really like to get to know, and it turns out she's inextricably married to some loser and you spend the next week wishing life had dealt the pack better and she had fallen into your lap instead of his? Well here she was, talking to me. I forgave Pedro in a moment.

"So you heard from my buddy Pedro?" I said.

Her smile faded. "Yes, and he gave me the sad news. My sympathies, what a dreadful thing! I gather Bruno was a good friend of yours?"

I nodded. "How well did you know him?"

"Not well. We met for the first time at Stan Rothman's last night."

"I'm trying to figure out the reason for that get-together," I said.

She smiled. ""I can't help you there because I've been wondering the same thing."

"Just social, then?"

She shook her head. "There's no such thing with Stan. He has a motive for everything."

"Usually financial?"

"Always financial."

I nodded. "I've been looking at the list of guests and trying to make sense of it. There were some allies and then there were also enemies of Rothman, if you want to put it like that."

"Which are you?"

"I wasn't there."

"The question still applies. Which are you?"

"Enemy, I guess you'd have to say."

"How come?"

"How much do you know?"

She wrinkled her brow. "Not much."

"Well, we crossed paths in Cuba last year. I was running a boatload of folk from Cuba to the Keys – I do that for a living. Bruno was my contact in Havana, his job being to assemble the refugees and bring them to a remote beach fifty miles from the city.

"The weather that night was favourable – calm, with a full moon. There were women and children and I was loading them onto the boat, using a rubber raft to get them across from the sand when all hell broke loose. The police arrived in force, and a coastguard boat with searchlights."

"Sounds scary."

"Averagely so. The entire boatload was arrested

including me, but with one exception, namely Martin Sanchez-Madera."

"There was a Martin at the party last night," she said.

"Same guy."

"He seemed nice."

"He is. He's also an enemy of the regime."

"The Castros?"

"And their system, which is still entrenched. Fidel died aged ninety-one but his brother Raúl, who is eighty-six, was President and is still secretary of the Communist party, the real centre of power."

"Sounds like there was a tipoff that Martin was on the boat," she said.

"Yes, and it was not a leak from me because until that night I had never heard of the guy."

"You say he escaped?"

"Right. He ran like hell into the dunes and they lost him, despite the searchlights."

"How come he's in Miami now?"

"Things were impossible for him in Cuba. He would have liked to stay – he was a professor of Political Science at the university in Havana and a candidate for leadership when the regime finally comes to an end, but he grabbed a ride on another boat and got out. He works in Miami now. He has a job lecturing at UM. They haven't made him a full professor but he's very much in demand, under-standably given his experience."

"We talked a bit. He seems smart," she said.

"He is."

She tossed her head and her blonde hair kissed her shoulders. "So the good guys at the party include him and me – and Bruno of course. As for bad guys, you'd have to include Rothman himself. Who does that leave as unknowns? I guess Rod Stirling and the Watts girls."

"You can put Stirling in with the baddies," I said.

"Why?"

I thought about my exchange with the singer that morning. "Trust me. Tell me about the Watts girls. Who are they?"

She smiled. "Twin sisters, British, plenty of money."

"What are they doing in Florida?"

"I'm not sure. Their father was a stockbroker or money manager, something like that, into offshore bank accounts and such. That's where the money comes from. They have a big house in Cocoplum."

Cocoplum is an expensive subdivision in Coral Gables. "Is their father based in Miami?"

"He died several years ago. And it's Antigua, he ran a hedge fund on Antigua."

"The girls inherited?"

"So I understand."

I scratched my chin. Realised I hadn't shaved. My five o'clock shadow starts around noon. "I guess I should pay them a visit, too."

She looked at me appraisingly. "They are good looking."

"Both of them?"

She nodded. "Identical twins."

I was out of questions. I got up to leave.

"What sort of medicine do you practice?" I asked.

She smiled. "Whole body health."

"Is that a specialty?" I asked.

"It is here."

"Sounds a bit vague. Is it covered by insurance?"

"Maybe. But I only deal with rich patients, frankly."

"It seems to provide a good living." I looked around the room, and out of the panoramic window across towards Key Biscayne. The distant Key was lapped by blue water and my view was framed by the reds, greens and yellows of downtown Miami's high-rise buildings. Miami is a colourful city, literally. When the drug boom hit in the days of Miami Vice and pastel linen suits, big money, much of it from offshore, went into transforming the look of the city with brightly coloured buildings. It's one big Mondrian canvas.

She laughed. "Yes, and I'm not ashamed of it."

She looked at me closely. "I doubt if you need my services, though, you look pretty fit."

"I think so too," I said. "But you're the expert."

"I'm a connoisseur of bodies and I like the general impression," she said.

"Thank you, ma'am."

"What are you, five eleven?"

I shook my head. "Six foot. People think I'm shorter because I have broad shoulders."

"Weight two hundred?"

"Soaking wet."

"Do you diet?"

"No. I eat a lot of black beans and rice – *Moros y Christianos.*"

"You're on the dark side. Swarthy in fact. And that suntan is cool. I'm not getting a clue from your name, are you Hispanic?"

I smiled and shook my head.

"Jewish?"

"Israeli," I said.

"Is there a difference?"

"It depends," I said. I was starting to feel self-conscious.

As I turned to leave she stretched out a hand and stroked my cheek with one finger, then leaned in and kissed me gently on the mouth.

I inhaled a faint whiff of scent. I don't know perfumes but I'm pretty sure hers was expensive.

Hmm. Two choices presented, maybe three: One, recoil. Not my style. Besides, it was a good kiss, so that choice was declined. Two, respond, slightly or wholeheartedly. That was tempting. The third choice was to smile enigmatically and file the incident away for future reference, which is what I chose to do.

A small voice said go for it, you could become good friends fast, but a second small voice, more insistent, whispered, "You don't know this woman, you only just met."

"Does that matter?" asked the first voice.

It might. She had called herself one of the good guys which she probably was, but what if . . .? I don't know if my smile was enigmatic or just goofy but for better or worse I flashed it, turned, and was back in the Jeep in moments, sinking rapidly in the vehicle elevator.

To buy FEAVER PITCH, go to GrahamTempest.com or to the store or website where you bought this book.

ACHNOWLEDGMENTS

Thanks so much to the advance readers who battled through the manuscript of Casino Havana. They will see from the many changes how valuable their work was.

Thanks too to peerless editor Sheryl Lee and brilliant designer Stuart Bache (cover.)

CASINO HAVANA is a work of fiction. Names, characters, places
and incidents either are the product of the author's imagination
or are used fictitiously and any resemblance to actual persons
living or dead, businesses, companies, events or locales is entirely
coincidental.

Cayo Piedra is a real island – you can look down on it using an
Internet mapping service – but I took a few liberties in terms of
what goes on there now. Only the Cuban government knows what
those buildings are really for.

Graham Tempest is a British-American author who divides his time between Oxfordshire and Florida.

grahamtempest.com